THE SKATEBOARD DETECTIVES

To Josh, Ed and Liam, who in one evening session at Bay66 got me back on board after a 25-year gap. Also, to all the gang at middle-aged-shred.com – Phil C., Bleary, Big Al, Joolz and Woody, who gave me hope that it's never too late to rock fakie! And final thanks to Penny, who had faith in the idea.

ORCHARD BOOKS
338 Euston Road, London NW1 3BH
Orchard Books Australia
Level 17/207 Kent Street, Sydney, 2000, NSW, Australia

First published in 2008 by Orchard Books
A paperback original

ISBN: 978 1 84616 607 5

Text © Andrew Fusek Peters 2008

The righ or of this
work yright,

A CIP ca sh Library

Orchard Hachette

THE SKATEBOARD DETECTIVES

Priceless!

ANDREW FUSEK PETERS

ORCHARD BOOKS

1. CHASE

'It's a dead end. We've got him now!'

Three men. One boy. No competition.

The lone figure was a hundred metres ahead of the three but the distance was already shrinking second by second.

The boy glanced back then pushed his skateboard faster. The click of the wheels echoed around the buildings.

They lost sight of him briefly in the fog, but there was nothing to worry about, nowhere for the lad to go. This alley led only one way – straight to the river. Under the bright neon streetlamps the cobbles shone from the recent rain. All the old buildings had been done up – huge wharves transformed into vast loft

5

apartments for rich city-boys with too much money. But who in their right mind would be out in the middle of a night like this, with the mist rising damp and humid from the river? No, this corner of the city was asleep. So much the better.

The fog parted for a few seconds and as the men slowed to a walking pace, closing in, the boy suddenly crouched down on the board with his right hand reaching for the cobbles. The next second, he slid deftly round in a circle and skidded to a stop. He stood up and stared at them defiantly.

'Is this what you're looking for?' he shouted. His other hand held up a memory stick glinting like pirate treasure.

Standing there, he looked like any typical thirteen-year-old: baggy jeans, sweatshirt, hoodie with the hood up. Nothing too original. The men paused for a moment, slightly uneasy. At this point the lad ought to be cowering and terrified. His actions didn't fit. But then the tallest one, the leader, smiled.

To most people, a smile from such a well-dressed young man would be appealing. But there was nothing polite in the sharp curve that creased this man's lips. The boy was obviously stupid. They would get what they came for. No doubt.

They advanced through the tendrils of mist, gently now, as if they were hunters flushing out a nervous deer.

The boy stared at them one more time, then winked, placed his board back down, turned and zoomed off straight towards the embankment wall.

'What the...?' The leader broke into a sprint and the others followed, picking up speed. At the edge of the embankment lay a pile of sand, spades, shovels and a Portaloo. A single plank leant at an angle against the wall and this is what the boy accelerated towards. One more push and he hit the bottom of it. The plank wobbled dangerously but held as he sped up and crouched down. He reached the top. Beyond lay nothing but a sheer drop. Suddenly the boy was airborne, flying out of the alleyway over the river wall. Then he plummeted. There was a splash. Then silence.

The other two were out of breath as they puffed and panted, leaning out over the low parapet to look down into the thick, rain-swollen waters. The leader had followed the boy's exact path up the plank and now stood on the wall, his hands cupped over his eyes like binoculars.

'There!' he gestured and they all saw it. An upturned skateboard floated away from them. With the lights of the city twisting and turning in the reflecting river, the scene looked almost pretty – inspiration for painters and poets. But they also saw the huge, bubbling swirls on the surface and knew and respected the water for its devious turns. No man, let alone a boy, could survive the strength of those undercurrents for more than a few seconds.

The leader stood on the wall like a statue. It bothered him. Why would the boy do such a thing? Maybe because he knew he was trapped, with no way out. Maybe... He looked down to make sure. The walls were smooth straight down to the water, except for an old, iron docking ring, rusting away. The time when the river had been used by barges going about their business was long gone. The leader shook his head, all doubt vanishing. By the time their little thief had been fished out, the memory stick would hold about as much information as a goldfish. Their secret was safe.

'Come on, boys. Our good friend the river has done our work for us, and we didn't even need to grease her palm.' The other two laughed. It was part of the job description to laugh at the leader's jokes. He jumped off the wall and stood expectantly, pointing to his turn-ups while one of them pulled out a pocket clothes-brush to clean the dirt from his trousers. The leader shrugged, smoothed his hair with one hand and with the other clicked his fingers impatiently. The three men turned away from the water and disappeared back into the night.

2. CHASE

Sunday 13 August, 2.30 am – the present

What chance did he have? The odds were against him. Three fit men against one boy and his board down a dead-end alley. His street wheels were hard as concrete, juddering. His dad still had a board from the 'old school' days. He was always going on about how the wheels were made for tarmac – 'bright green Sims Snakes, the smoothest ride in town'. As the boy's frame bumped and shook over the cobbles, he thought how he could have done with that ride right now.

Mind you, he'd led them a merry race for the last twenty minutes, zipping in and out of streets, underpasses and junctions. He hoped it would give the gang enough time.

This had better be the right alley! he thought.

Or I'm dead... The mist was perfect, almost like he'd ordered it. Good! There was the plank, thirty metres ahead. He crouched down, leant over and put his right hand down on the glistening cobblestones to execute a perfect one-hundred-and-eighty-degree power slide. From full speed to a full stop, facing his three hunters. He needed to buy a bit of time, stop them in their tracks, make them think he was dumb. The memory stick was in his pocket. And if they thought he had all the information on it, the information to buy one man's freedom, well, that was the point of the whole exercise.

'Is this what you're looking for?'

The taunting worked. He liked the pause in their stride, the momentary uncertainty that crossed the leader's face, a face he wouldn't forget: the blond hair slicked back, the cold blue of the eyes and the diamond stud in the left ear.

They reckoned they had him now. And because they had him, there was no hurry. They were off-balance, lazy, just where he wanted them. He could feel the adrenalin rushing through his body as he smiled inanely at them. Time for action. He slipped the stick back into his pocket and was off. He pumped the pavement with his left foot. Goofy-footed, the other skaters called him. If only they could see him now. The plank was straight in front of him. He had to hit it just right. A few centimetres either side and he'd slam straight into the wall. Then he was cruising up, terrified, nothing between him and the murderous currents. How could you rehearse something like that? You couldn't. A plan was only a plan. This was the real thing.

At the last second, as the board was itching to leave the embankment wall and hurtle into the sky, he crouched down. Yes. His fingers fumbled, but it was there, loosely tucked under the top of the plank. The end of the rope. In one swift movement, he looped it around his wrist and locked on, hoping that just this once the laws of physics were correct. He stood up and kicked back on the tail and the board literally ricocheted off the embankment wall. It was an Ollie better than the great Alan 'Ollie' Gelfand himself had ever managed. He took off diagonally, defying gravity. But this was one landing his kit would not make with him. The board slipped away from his feet and arced through the air, away and down. He registered the splash, hoped it was loud enough to sound like a body hitting water.

The boy also flew, a projectile without wings,

straight out over the water, with the only line between him and drowning wrapped thin and frayed around his forearm. The rope pulled taut, almost dislocating his shoulder. At the other end, the docking ring it looped around lifted off the wall and strained. Time slowed down. The boy mentally crossed his fingers. Who knows how many years since that ring had held back the weight of a barge full of coal against the unending current of the river? Fortune was kind, though, and the ring did its job as it clenched the rope that swung him in a graceful semi-circle, down and down and straight towards the wall.

The boy had no desire to learn what it was like to be squashed flat like a pizza. If the rope was too long or short, well, forget it. But there it was, looming like a big, black open mouth. He never thought he'd feel so much affection for a sewage outfall. He could practically have kissed it. A blink of an eye and he swung like Tarzan straight into the tunnel mouth, slipping on his bum through all-too-identifiable slime. There wasn't a moment to lose. His right arm was killing him, but nothing seemed broken. He quickly unknotted himself and pulled one end of the rope to slip it off the docking ring and drag it into the tunnel. Evidence. All that blue-eyes would see now was a rusty ring. He hoped that nobody would start to put two and two together.

Someone shouted. 'There!'

The boy froze. Maybe they'd spotted him. Then he flicked his eyes towards the river. He spotted the board and his heart ached. Toy Machine deck, Indy 129 trucks and a nice set of Spitfires with Swiss bearings... What a waste of a great bit of kit. You win some, you lose some. Voices murmured above him. If one of them leant over far enough, they could spot this place, easy. It was a gamble. Still, it would take them a while to work out how to get down a vertical wall slippery with green stuff. He'd be gone into the bowels of the city long before then. He strained his ears, listening hard, so when the voices came to their conclusion and drifted off into the darkness, he allowed himself to breathe again.

Yes! Yes! Yes! He clenched his fist up at the ceiling of the tunnel. Oh yes! He, the boy known as Break to his mates, had done it. It was the stunt to beat all stunts, and not a camcorder in sight. Life was so unfair.

Break pushed his hood back. Underneath, he was wearing the latest high-beam caving headgear. He pressed a switch and the tunnel was flooded with light. It was made of brick that might once have been red but was now stained with the contents of two hundred years of organic human matter. It was about three metres high and perfectly circular apart from a channel cut in the bottom to ease the flow.

'Yeeuch!' He didn't want to look at his feet. And he certainly didn't want to think about what was soaking through his Etnies right now.

When he'd been researching his getaway, he'd found out that the supposedly solid city stood on a honeycombed layer of buried rivers, Tube tunnels and a spaghetti of sewers. He studied the blackness ahead of him. This ancient river was long buried. Where once children fished along the banks and laundrywomen laid out their white linen, rats now scampered, and if there were any fish Break had no desire to meet them. He tied the rope around his waist and slowly began to walk up the tunnel.

Ahead of him the tunnel split into two. He pulled out his iPod and worked the click wheel. You could download anything these days. A few minutes of surfing and he'd come across an underground A–Z. It wasn't as if he could stop someone and ask the way, unless the rats that brushed against his feet had suddenly acquired the ability to speak.

Break took a left. Instead of sloshing along in a few centimetres of water, the filthy stream was suddenly lapping at his ankles. It also felt like he was under a particularly revolting shower, as his headlamp picked out thousands of grey-brown stalactites stuck to the brick arch overhead, each one dripping in a constant rhythm. He'd be glad to get out, that was for sure. But what was that other sound? The hum that had been lurking in the background for a while grew louder. He put his hand against one of the bricks and could feel it vibrating. Tube train? Traffic above, filtering down? Not at this time of night.

He quickened his pace. Weaving left and right through the forks, he steadily worked his way uphill. The flow was nearly up to his knees now and it was slow going. At least the smell had gone. This water was silty brown, with the look of a swollen river. Something niggled in his mind, something he had read. The rivers of the city had long gone to sleep, but when the rains came, they would sometimes wake up again. That was it. This passage wasn't just a sewer. It was a storm sewer. And the summer rains had been going on for three days. Not good.

He knew he ought to be close to the meeting

place, so he began anxiously scanning the curving walls for the metal rungs that should be there.

The hum turned up in volume. He rounded a corner and the tunnel headed straight as a Roman road into the darkness. His lamp caught the rusty metal rungs only thirty metres ahead of him. Great! But the current was strong and he was already wading up to his waist. Still, not far, just very wet. He had the beam of light trained on the ladder, but when the angry hum suddenly switched to an ominous roar he jerked his head around. The lamp confirmed what he'd been dreading. The surge of water that powered towards him out of the darkness was no joke.

Every stream for miles around, every drop that soaked into the ground had been funnelled by engineers to create a monster wave now swallowing everything in its path and accelerating second by second. If he'd had his surfboard it could have been the ride of a lifetime. But as it was, he had no choice except to struggle furiously towards the ladder as the water swelled under his armpits and the wave came crashing towards him.

There were only two thoughts in his head. The

first was: ladder. The second was that he'd just duped one of the top gangs in the city only to be finished off by the jolly old British weather. There really was no justice.

3. BREAK AND ENTER

Sunday 13 August, 1.30 am – one hour earlier

'You must be kidding! How do you expect me to get up there?' Sanjay looked up at the two sheer walls that met at a right angle. It didn't help that he barely came up to Ben's shoulder.

'Listen, little San, it's just a matter of technique. That's all. Remember, my mum was a gymnast and I've been at this since I was a kid.' Ben paced the distances, working the whole thing out. His tall, rangy body was a pressed coil, ready to spring with every step. Even the short dreads that he sported looked bouncy.

'Anyway, this bit is Ben's job,' said Charlie. 'He gets us up, I get us in, and then San, we let you loose on the computers!'

Sanjay shrugged his shoulders. The word

'little' bugged him. Just because Ben was a beanpole in the making, he didn't need to rub it in. Still, at least it was better than some of the other nicknames he got at school.

Break stood to one side, lost in his own thoughts, but his eyes were sharp as he kept lookout. It was too late for the late-night drunks, too early for the street-sweepers. The city had well and truly gone to beddy-byes – the perfect time for a bit of building infiltration.

Ben was ready. He glanced up. 'Oh great. Anyone spot the camera?' There was no such thing as a blind corner in a place like this. Whatever it was that lay inside was clearly intended to stay that way. A frown creased Ben's face.

'The great *Dread*-ded Ben himself is put out! Thinks we've slipped up? One up to me, I reckon!' Sanjay wagged a finger at Ben and pulled out his PDA. 'And here's one I prepared earlier: my personal digital assistant. Or, as I like to think of it, a friend in need. The inbuilt satellite receiver intercepts the digital video stream and does a little loop-the-loop. Thanks to my wireless talents, current camera is presently looking at the same empty scene over and over again. It's the oldest trick in the book. But a security guard on five quid an hour is more interested in the footy than a camera showing the latest series of *Empty Space*!' Sanjay gave a little bow as Ben punched him on the shoulder.

'Wow. I knew you were into computers, but how'd you afford this kind of stuff?' asked Break, glancing back briefly before returning his gaze to lookout.

'You're not jealous, are you?' said San.

'No! Just asking.'

'Well, apart from doing IT consultancy, my dad sidelines by reviewing the latest gear for *Gizmoid*.'

'What, the gadget mag? Cool!'

'Yeah, and even cooler than that, the stuff is out of date a week later and all those freebies get passed on to yours truly. I am one techno-happy bunny! Plus, Dad's often so stuck in his computer all night, he's not likely to notice the temporary absence of his only child. Makes it easier to get out and about...'

'Well, gadgets are one thing, clever clogs. But now let me show you some *real* talent!' Ben crouched down and ran straight at the right-hand wall. At the last second, he leapt up, leading with his right leg. His foot met the wall, bent like a spring and bounced his body back to the second wall, which he struck with his left foot. He ricocheted across before reaching up to catch hold of the ledge four metres up. He pulled himself onto it, swivelled round and smiled down at the gang. 'Spider-Man, eat your heart out!'

'That was amazing!' Charlie knew that Ben was one of the best free-runners around, but this confirmed it. He made going up that wall look like taking a stroll along the pavement.

'It's all in the angles, girl! But a compliment from you will go a long way! Now come on, the rest of you!' Ben leant over the edge and with a lot of foot-holding and climbing on shoulders, the rest of the gang were soon standing on an area of flat roof. From the front, the building was a wall of tinted black glass, anonymous, doing its best not to stand out from the other business premises that filled up this part of town. But around the back was where the messy business of architecture was revealed: heating ducts, air-conditioning units and plenty of pigeon droppings. There was a small window set into a wall right above a silver, curved heating cowl that particularly interested Charlie.

'Here we go!' she said, pointing out the way in.

'You've been watching too many movies!' hissed Sanjay. 'I'm not slithering down a heating duct!'

'No, stupid. The window!' Charlie slipped out a thin, metal ruler from the tool belt strapped around her waist. Her dad's kit. It was usually hidden beneath a floorboard in the attic as her dad had sworn to put his thieving days behind him. But he was the whole reason she was here. She was determined to prove him innocent. And if this was what it took, well, she hoped he'd be proud.

She leapt onto the heating duct and leant against the window. Sometimes, people were stupid. They'd use the most expensive alarm systems but forget to lock a window. She slipped the ruler in between the pane and frame, moved it around expertly and, hey presto! The catch was off and the thin rectangle of frosted glass swung up easily. The smell that wafted out told her that she had hit loo central.

'Oh great!' she muttered.

Ben was suddenly by her side, peering into the darkness. 'Give me a nice, easy wall any day! How are you going to get into there?' Ben's head would have fitted through, just, but as for shoulders and body, the opening was far too small.

'Watch and learn, Ben!' But Charlie didn't feel confident at all. The endless circus classes ever since she was little meant that wriggling in and out of tiny hoops was second nature. It helped that she was small for a twelve-year-old too. But as for a minute window, in pitch dark, with the potential for being flushed head first down the pan? She balanced her feet on the duct and pushed against the frame. No. Her shoulders were too wide. There was only one thing to do. For once, being younger (and smaller) than the others was a benefit.

There was a small popping sound. Ben was closest and his eyes went wide. 'That's disgusting...and...cool!' Charlie wasn't listening. Dislocating her right shoulder had given her the extra millimetres she needed, though the pain was another matter. Now she was a human snake, wriggling through the hole, flopping down on the (thankfully closed) loo seat. She wanted to scream as the whole right side of her body was on fire, but instead she balanced on the seat, turned around and guided her floppy arm back through the window.

'Pull, Ben, and be quick about it!' she hissed. Ben leant into the window and grabbed hold of her hand, tugging hard. She gritted her teeth as the bones ground together. Another pop, and she was back to normal again.

'Not bad for a twelve-year-old!' whispered Ben.

'And being one year older makes all the difference? I bow down to your superior wisdom!'

Ben put his hands up in the air as if to surrender. 'Fair play, girl!'

Charlie rubbed her shoulder and headed off, pulling on the infra-red goggles that Break had given her.

The loos were deserted, as was the corridor, apart from the criss-cross of ankle-height laser beams flaring bright red in Charlie's lenses. She hopped gingerly from blank space to blank space, gradually making her way round to an open door that led to an open-plan office. Clear. She ran to the window, undid the catch and leant out.

'Come on, slowcoaches. We haven't got all night!'

The rest of the gang bundled in, apart from Break, who passed out the other pairs of goggles.

Sanjay was the last to go in. 'OK, Break, now I've got some pretty nifty gear myself, but where do *you* get hold of this kind of stuff?'

'Easy,' Break smiled. 'Ex-military, courtesy of eBay. You just need to know where to look. I thought about getting a jet fighter as well, but there's nowhere to park it at our place.'

'Very good!'

Break got back to business. 'Have you reset the CCTV?' Sanjay nodded. 'Remember to put your phone on vibrate, and good luck!' Break crawled back to the edge of the wall and took up position to wait behind the CCTV camera. Sanjay and the others made their way into the depths of the building, creeping and leaping like puppets on strings through the spider's web of beams. No alarms went off, no trip-wires tripped. Easy-peasy. Down a stairwell, Sanjay consulted his PDA. 'Just to the right and along that passage should be the one,' he whispered.

They clustered around a featureless door. No handle. No lock. Only a six-figure keypad. Sanjay pulled out a small powder compact with a fluffy powder puff.

'I didn't know you took so much pride in your appearance,' Ben whispered.

'Do I look stupid?' Sanjay dusted the powder lightly over the keypad before squinting through the goggles. 'Odd...no fingerprints. No wear or tear on the buttons.' He thought for a second then muttered to himself, 'That's clever, that is. Let's have a little look around, shall we?' A few metres away, there was a large coiled-up fire hose attached to the wall, and above it, a fire alarm. A printed sign warned passers-by that it was 'For Emergency Use Only'. 'Hmmm...' Sanjay peered closely at the red button. 'I wonder...' He dusted it with the powder puff, as before. 'Bingo!' A perfect fingerprint was illuminated by everyone's goggles. With a gulp, he held his finger over the button.

'No way, San! You're not pressing that thing! Are you mad?' Ben jumped towards Sanjay, aiming to knock his hand away, but he was too late. Sanjay had pressed the button.

'Oh, my...' Charlie breathed, but there was nothing, no shrieking bell, only a small click. Then, slowly and silently, the coiled hose swung away from them, inwards, revealing a dark gap in the wall.

'Result!' Ben patted Sanjay on the shoulder. They were in.

Inside, the room was a box with no windows and no doors – apart from the half-height, hidden entrance through which they had crept in. In the middle stood a desk with a computer, the screensaver's blue waves criss-crossing the surface. Sanjay stepped straight towards it. There was a sudden, shrill clamouring. An alarm! Charlie's eyes widened as she turned to Ben. The sound was deafening. There was no time to lose.

'Behind the desk, quick.' Sanjay turned and pushed the other two ahead of him, felt in his pocket for his phone and pushed the 'send' button. Within seconds they heard the clatter of boots up the corridor. Sanjay crossed his fingers. The lights were still off and they could see the sweep of a torchlight through the gap in the wall. Three rats trapped in a cage.

On the flat roof, Break felt his phone vibrate. He scrabbled over the far edge of the wall and nearly broke his ankles as he hit the hard ground. He retrieved his board from a bush, gave a long and, he hoped, fearful look up at the CCTV camera, and then set off slowly on his board.

'Come on!' he muttered to himself. 'Get a move on, guys!'

The guards paused outside the computer-room door and one of them got on his hands and knees to crawl in. The torch beam lit up the wall behind the hidden kids. Surely he'd see them. A walkie-talkie on the guard's belt crackled into life.

'We have a visual on the intruder. Repeat. We have a visual on the intruder. Exiting west of the building and onto Caledonian Road. He must be stopped!' The man immediately crawled backwards through the hole, banging his head in the process. Footsteps vanished into the distance. Sanjay smiled and breathed again. The plan had worked!

Charlie crawled to the edge of the hole and peered out carefully. The corridor was deserted. She stuck her thumb in the air to Sanjay, who pulled out his memory stick and set to work straightaway.

'USB. Whack it in the back of the computer. A few seconds to install the key-logger program and every single thing typed in the past twenty-four hours, down to the last full stop, is mine!' Sanjay was in his element. His fingers flew as he searched the saved file for repeated words. Within seconds, this gave him the password. *It was just like the door to this room!* he thought. *Everything had a solution.*

'Well, San,' nodded Charlie, 'you may not be the brawniest kid on the block, but your brain is seriously fit!'

Ben, however, hated tiny spaces. He paced up and down the room nervously. 'You know what? This whole thing is mad. We're school pupils, not professionally trained spooks! I mean, if we get caught, it's not like getting a detention...'

Charlie put a hand on Ben's shoulder. 'Look, I'm sorry I got you all into this. But the police are no use to us while they're still after my dad, so it's up to us. We got this far. Please don't let me down now.'

'Yeah, yeah,' said Ben, though his whole body quivered with tension.

The alarm was suddenly turned off so that the only sound was the rhythm of Sanjay's fingers tap-dancing over the keys. The screen was a whirring blur of figures as the hard disk coughed up its secrets.

'Look!' said Sanjay. Ben turned and instantly forgot his fear. The screen showed a photo of an egg. An egg unlike any they had ever seen. It glittered and shone, illuminating the face of the man holding it proudly in his hands. It was a handsome face, with cold blue eyes, slicked-back blond hair and a diamond stud in the left ear. The image flickered and was gone, copied onto the key. Sanjay snapped it out and slipped it into his pocket: the key to saving another man's life.

They crawled out through the hole and strolled back the way they had come. The laser beams had been switched off. After all, why look for another set of thieves when you're chasing one? According to logic, Sanjay, Ben and Charlie didn't even exist. They were safe to leave. It was all down to Break now.

4. THE OFFER

Saturday 29 July, 7.00 pm – two weeks earlier

Danny Cooper was shattered. He'd just got off the long-distance coach and was making his way home. It was two weeks since he'd seen his wife and his daughter, Charlie; two weeks on a gas platform in the middle of the sea cooking three meals a day. For the lads on shift it was no problem – twelve hours on, twelve hours off. But if he didn't deliver a decent spaghetti carbonara or their steak just how they liked it, there was nowhere to run to: not unless he wanted to dive a hundred metres down into the North Sea. And the helicopter journey back to land killed his appetite stone dead every time.

When he'd been let out of jail, his probation officer had set him up with a careers interview.

He'd been expecting the usual put-downs and an offer to work in the local DIY store, stacking shelves. But when he'd mentioned how he'd loved cooking as a young lad, the woman's eyes lit up. As far as she was concerned, Danny Cooper, former safe-breaker extraordinaire, was a challenge. Within two weeks he'd been signed up for an access course at the local college, hanging out with students half his age. But he'd made good progress and was soon apprenticed in a local restaurant. When the offer of work in the middle of the North Sea turned up, a steady wage was just too good to refuse.

The worst bit had been the safety course. They had actually strapped him into a mock-up helicopter and lowered him upside down into the bottom of a very deep swimming pool. Sheer fear got him out of that one... Still, two months on and he was earning a real salary. Life looked interesting once again.

The sun was low and made his shadow stretch out along the street. At least he'd be home soon. Charlie appreciated the effort he was making, and as for his wife...well. As long as she had her Fred Astaire and Ginger Rogers musicals on DVD, she'd be fine.

Danny tightened the belt on his rucksack and

quickened his pace. Rush hour was over and the street seemed too quiet. He heard a car behind him. An instinct from the old days made him turn. It was a black Mercedes, polished to ridiculous lengths, with mirrored windows, fat tyres and an out-of-place rear spoiler. It didn't click. He must have been really tired.

'Alright, Danny? Long time no see.' A window rolled down and a sweaty face peered out.

'Is that you, Piggy?'

The face fell. 'Don't call me that or I'll...'

'Twirl your tail...I know!' Danny smiled while the other man went red in the face.

'One day, Danny Cooper. One day...!' The man shook his gloved fist. 'Now get in the back as our man wants a word with you.'

Rule one about black Mercedes cars with tinted windows: there's never just one suited scumbag crawling out of the sewer, but a whole family. Danny sighed.

'Don't suppose I have much choice about that, do I?'

The door was opened and he slid reluctantly onto the leather seat.

'I *am* impressed, Mr Cooper. Cooking up real meals instead of the latest recipe for gelignite. Does this mean you're a changed man?' The face was in shadow but the voice was unmistakeable.

'Evening, Vince. Thought I'd bump into you sooner or later.'

The voice spoke again. 'Seems a shame not to catch up, talk about old times.'

Danny stayed silent as they pulled up outside a pub. Piggy leapt out and held the door open. The other bodyguard, Dirk, slipped out of the car and accompanied them. Piggy scuttled round them again and held the pub door open as if he was ushering in royalty.

Danny was always amazed at Vince's ability to enter a room. It was just like one of those old westerns. The gang entered and the whole pub fell silent. The publican nodded at Vince and half-finished conversations were allowed to resume.

'Don't you get bored giving everyone the frights, Vince?'

Vince pulled at the cuffs on his shirt and smoothed down the front of his suit. The blue eyes locked on him. 'Never. It's always good to know where you stand, eh?'

Piggy planted himself meaningfully next to a table occupied by a young couple. They broke off from canoodling to realise that they were being stared at by a thug in a suit and gloves and they quickly got the message, fleeing like startled rabbits. Piggy wiped the table with his coat sleeve and indicated for the others to sit down.

'Diet Coke, isn't it, Danny? You've put down the drink.'

'If you're trying to impress me with your knowledge, Vince, I've heard it all before. And yes, with lemon and ice...please.'

Vince clicked his fingers and Piggy brought the drink over. He lifted the bottle and poured it into the glass. The Coke frothed up. 'Oops, shouldn't have shaken the bottle. Tee hee!'

'Love the gloves, Piggy! Fashion statement? Or the old eczema giving you trouble?' said Danny as he took a sip. Piggy tried his most murderous stare but it simply made him look like a cross-eyed toddler.

Vince pulled out a sheet of paper and unfolded it. It was a photograph of an egg.

'Seen one of these before?'

'Is this a test or something?'

'No, just want to see if standing at a red-hot stove has addled your brains.'

Danny picked up the piece of paper and pulled it closer. He sighed. 'A right beauty, that is...'

'Go on...'

'The perfect gift for the tsar who has

35

everything. The year is 1898 and this is the latest in a series of Easter gifts, from the house of Fabergé. This one is...that's it! Lilies of the Valley – pink enamel, covered in pearls. Pink was the Empress's favourite colour...'

'You always were one of the best thieves, Danny. A little knowledge goes a long, long way,' Vince smiled.

Danny was lost in the picture now. 'The amazing bit about it is when you push the tiny crown at the top – the whole egg opens out like a flower to reveal three painted oval miniatures of Tsar Nicholas II and his two daughters, Olga and Tatiana. A jewelled gadget...that's what it is.'

Vince bent over and whispered in Danny's ear, 'And I want you to steal it for me.'

Danny sat back. 'There was always something about the portraits that bugged me. You know, come 1918, they were all led into a basement and shot, the whole family. This egg's got blood all over it...'

'Nothing like a good story to increase the value,' Vince continued, ignoring him. 'Now listen, the oil billionaire Yevtushenko is lending his private set of nine eggs to the Gilbert Collection, right here in London at Somerset House. Security is unbelievable, but that's never deterred you. The exhibition opens next week, but inside sources tell me the egg is already there. This should be a piece of cake for the great Danny Cooper.'

Danny pushed his Coke bottle away. He suddenly felt a bit queasy. 'You're mad!'

Piggy looked as if he wanted to strangle him.

Vince's eye twitched. 'Don't ever say that. Ever!' he hissed.

'I'm straight now. You let me take the fall for that last bank job and never even gave me my share when I came out. What do *I* owe *you*?'

'The money was invested. It's all there for you and a nice ten per cent cut of this job, if you do it.'

'Are you kidding? Do I look like I want Scotland Yard and half the Russian mafia on my tail? No. I might not make much, but at least it's honestly earned. I owe it to my daughter.'

There was a moment of silence. Piggy looked from Danny to Vince and back again while shaking his head.

BANG! Vince smashed his hand on the table. The whole pub jumped. Danny had no desire to be on the other end of Vince's fist.

'Fair enough,' said Vince, almost in a whisper. 'We just wanted to ask you, for old times' sake. I guess we have to go to Plan B.' Vince smiled unexpectedly, as if the whole thing was just a bit of a wheeze and no hard feelings, eh?

Danny stood up and pulled his rucksack on. The pub seemed to go a funny shape for a moment. He really needed to get out of there. He searched for the exit and swayed towards it, slamming the door open. Fresh air. He wondered for a second why Piggy wasn't coming after him. It wasn't like Vince. It wasn't like him at all. And what did he mean by Plan B? The egg was pretty, though.

'Pretty little egg, I love you so!' he began to sing. The streetlamps danced with him. Danny missed his footing and fell. Then everything went black.

5. NOT ALL IT'S CRACKED UP TO BE

Sunday 30 July, 10.00 am – next morning

'Dad! Dad! Wake up, will you?' Charlie kept shaking the prone body. There were tears in her eyes. Last night, she'd tidied the whole house and sorted Mum out with her favourite TV dinner in front of a new edition of *Singin' in The Rain*. Later, chores done, she'd sat in the kitchen by herself, waiting as dusk fell. Finally, long after the coach was due in, she'd slipped past the living room and the glow under the door, and gone out into the street. Typical Dad! How could she have believed his promise? He was probably down the pub right now, swilling down his family's money. And he'd sworn everything would change...

She'd peered in every pub window between

home and the coach station, but all she'd seen was a fug of smoke and smeary faces staring back at her. It was after ten when she'd spotted a slumped figure in a shop doorway. She knew it was him immediately. Thank the gods for all her circus training. He was passed out cold, so the balancing act of getting a body twice her weight all the way home hadn't exactly been easy. His eyes were all funny and bloodshot and he kept singing about Humpty Dumpty falling to pieces until she managed to drag him upstairs and cover him with a blanket.

Why couldn't she have a normal family? She was more grown up than both of them. Charlie sighed and pulled the curtains open, revealing bright sunlight.

'Mmmmff,' her dad grunted.

'You were drunk!' said Charlie, slamming a cup of tea (two sugars) down on the bedside table.

'No...no.' Danny flailed his arms around as if he was an octopus, an octopus who was going bald and getting too old for all this. Where was he? He remembered making his way down the street and then...nothing. 'I didn't...honestly, don't know what happened.'

'Huh. I do. A quick half on the way home and magically, the drinks multiply, and suddenly

I find you half-asleep in a doorway. Strange though...' she paused, thinking back, 'don't remember the smell of drink on your breath...'

'Sorry, doll. Really am.' Danny sat up in bed and took a sip of tea. 'Great cuppa.'

'Oh, Dad!' She came and gave him a hug. 'Here's the paper. No doubt you were singing with your mates when this happened!' Charlie stabbed her finger at the headline.

Fabergé Egg Stolen in Daring Raid

Danny put his hand to a head that threatened to split in half. It was all coming back to him. 'Oh no! I don't believe it.'

Charlie's eyes narrowed. 'You didn't have anything to do with this, did you?'

'Never. Look at the state of me. Come on, Charlie, give me a break!' He hunched forwards and began to read.

Brute force and extreme cunning were used last night to steal one of the rarest Fabergé eggs in existence: the celebrated Lilies of the Valley egg.

Part of a collection of nine eggs being loaned by a Russian oil billionaire for a two-week exhibition at Somerset House, the Lilies of the Valley egg was to have been a closely guarded, surprise exhibit at a star-studded event. However, as the egg was being delivered to the launch party of the new fragrance 'Pink' by Squitney Leers, a traffic diversion led the armoured van down a one-way alley. As soon as the van stopped, a gang of three blew the door open with explosives and forced the guards out. One security guard has multiple injuries from the blast and is still in intensive care...

'That's such a crude way of doing things!' muttered Danny, under his breath. He put the paper down, sighing and rubbing his eyes. So Vince had already had the whole thing planned by early yesterday evening. What on earth was going on? Danny had no idea. 'How's your mother?' he asked instead.

'You know. As long as she can set the hard-disk recorder and get all the daytime Fifties films, she's just fine!'

Danny winced as he remembered the cheerful girl he'd married. Maybe if he hadn't got caught that last time...

'It's not your fault, Dad. We got along okay, the

last two weeks. But I'm glad you're back.'

'Me too, doll. Let me have a shower, look in on your mum and then we'll go out and get ourselves a really good fry-up, eh? I can tell you all about life on the high seas.'

Charlie couldn't help but smile. Her dad might have been a chancer but when he was home she felt that all was right with the world.

All was not right with the world two mornings later, however. At 7.30 am there was a sharp knock on the door. Charlie was already up, sorting out some porridge for her mum. She peered through the frosted glass at the two figures behind. It was too early for the milkman. She kept the chain on and undid the latch.

'Police. Is your dad home?' A man and a woman in uniform stood on the doorstep. The man did the talking while sniffing in a way that suggested the house was a rats' nest of criminal intent.

Charlie wasn't going to give in that easily. 'Show us your ID, then!'

'Don't be cheeky, girl!'

'It's called *rights*, actually. I thought you lot knew the law.'

The man's face flushed red. He fumbled in his

43

pocket. 'Fine. Here. Why would we want to get up this early to imitate a couple of cops, eh?'

Charlie reluctantly undid the latch and let them in, shouting upstairs at the same time. She showed them into the kitchen and deliberately didn't offer them a cup of tea even though the male officer kept looking pointedly at the kettle. She hoped her mum wouldn't make one of her rare appearances downstairs.

After a couple of minutes, her dad came in, pulling up the zip on his jeans and tucking in his shirt.

'Why, it's the great Danny Cooper, in the flesh. I ought to ask you for your autograph. Though on second thoughts, maybe not.' This cop obviously thought he was the bee's knees. The female officer, who had heard it all before, inspected her nails.

'What do you want?' Danny asked.

'Well, we didn't come all this way for a cup of tea. Though I wouldn't say no to one. Mind telling us what you were doing on Saturday night, say between 8.00 and 10.00 pm?'

Charlie tried to hide the shock in her face but she saw her dad's eyes narrow. 'Why are you asking?' He turned away from them while he put the kettle on but she could see the shake of his hands.

'Come on, Danny. We haven't got all day, have we. I mean, an egg worth millions goes walk-a-bye and the one and only Danny Cooper knows *nothing* about it?' The cop was enjoying his sarcasm.

'Strange though, all that violence – you don't normally hurt the punters, do you? I guess prison has hardened you after all!' The policeman paused. 'Still haven't answered my question...Danny?'

'I was...I got a bit drunk I guess.'

'Did you now? Was that a celebration – job well done, a few drinks for your mates sort of thing? And which pub exactly? They might help us with your alibi...'

'I don't...' Danny scratched his head but the whole evening was a blur. He looked defeated. 'I don't know.'

"Course you don't!' the cop smiled. 'And not only that, but some careless dummy left a Coke bottle at the scene. Theft is thirsty work, as they say. Even better than that: it has your prints all over it!' The policeman delivered the last line and practically took a bow when he'd finished.

Charlie wasn't sure which one she wanted to strangle first: him or her dad.

Danny bunched his fists. 'No way. I'm telling you. No way! I've been set up.' Danny looked pleadingly at his daughter.

The policewoman decided she was bored with her fingernails. 'They all say that, you know. Anyway, you're obviously desperate to get back to a prison cell.'

'I'd better get my coat, then.' Resigned, Danny left the kitchen and Charlie stared at the intruders, thinking hard about the sequence of events. There was an awkward silence before she burst out, 'My dad's innocent! He's got a job. He's straight now! My mum's been through hell and now that it's all good again, you want to spoil it.' She found herself crying and felt ashamed for showing this weakness.

'Sorry, love,' said the WPC. 'Just doing our job. Is there anyone to look after you?'

Charlie certainly wasn't going to let on about her mum. 'Yeah. No worries. Mum's not well, she's having a day off today...' (Every day was a day off for her mother but that was none of their business.)

Danny came back in and gave Charlie a hug. 'Listen. Don't you worry about me. I'll be fine. And I promise the truth will out, OK?'

For once, she believed him. He was taken by

the arm and led out of the house. The policeman pushed Danny's head down to duck into the waiting car and the doors slammed. Several neighbours stood in their front gardens and stared.

'It's not the circus, you know!' Charlie shouted and ran back inside. At least it was the summer holidays. Her classmates taunting her and teachers treating her with suspicion would have been too much.

Her dad had said, 'The truth will out...' But now the only person who could find out the truth was her. However, she couldn't do it alone. She took the cordless phone off the stand in the hallway and retreated to her bedroom. If anyone could help, it was the gang.

6. BREAKOUT!

Wednesday 2 August, afternoon

Charlie stood and surveyed the scene. When this concrete monstrosity had been built in the 1950s, for some reason it had been balanced on a whole load of pillars. In between the pillars, open to the elements, was a set of paved areas and banks with metal railings at the top. By night it was an ideal tramp hotel and by day the skaters could take over this perfect basement skate park. The authorities had tried for years to move everyone on, but had given up the fight. After all, it was paradise for wheels: smooth surfaces, great angles, and all protected from the elements.

There were a few skaters in this afternoon, plus the odd BMXer snaking in. Mostly boys...typical!

With her short haircut, she could almost pass as one herself – no one gave her a second glance. The whole gang was there, but Break was the one on edge, waiting for a gap between the constant click-clack of wheels. His board was on the ground, almost with a life of its own, raring to go while he hid inside his hoodie. Ben and Sanjay were talking about the latest PlayStation game, but when the hush fell and Break began pumping the board, they turned to look.

He was about ten metres from the metre-high railing and gaining speed. On the other side, the bank dropped at forty degrees to the flat basement. Just before the railing, Break kicked back and ollied into the air. Charlie was always amazed when Break took off. It was as close to flying as you could get without wings. In a flash, he was soaring high over the railing. But the smirk on his face said that was just for starters. At the peak of his ascent, he flipped the board over and right round, a perfect three-hundred-and-sixty-degree kickflip, connecting his feet back with the board to slam onto the ground and screech to a halt.

The gang had seen it before, but the other skaters slammed their decks on the ground in praise.

'Hmm!' said Ben, doing some stretches and warm-ups. 'How to follow that? A monkey or an underbar?'

'What is it with boys and their obsessions?' said Charlie. 'Is there some free-running boffin who comes up with these ridiculous code words?'

Ben did his best to look offended. 'It's called *parkour*, actually! And just 'cause you can't do it, there's no need to be sarky. I rehearse all these moves. It should be recognised as a sport, right? And what's more, most of the time we don't put down poncy landing mats like you soft gymnasts!' Ben loped off towards the railing and after three strides leapt into the air, swinging forwards feet first. Charlie always thought the move should be called the post-box as it was just like slotting a letter into a box. He slid through the railing without even touching the sides, flew over the bank and forward-rolled his way back to standing. The echo of fifty decks slapped on the bank, mixed in with wild cheers. The other skaters were getting a free show and were happy to play at being an audience.

Sanjay stared at Charlie. 'You're not going to put up with these two, are you?'

'Why don't you go, San?'

San pretended to think for a minute. 'Nah.

Jumping kerbs is about as exciting as it gets for me. Though in a hacking race, we know who'd win, eh?'

'Yeah, yeah...' said Charlie. She was already distracted. She'd come here to talk about her father, not take on the competition. Oh well. She studied the angles for a second, pacing them out in her head. This wasn't her local gym, but it would do. Her mind focused and she ran at the railing. At the very last moment, instead of leaping over it, she grabbed it with her right hand and spun herself up into a twirling one-handed handstand. As she let go, the momentum pushed her out and up. The timing was perfect as she began to both roll and twist like a corkscrew in mid-air. Elastic bands had nothing on this girl. She came out of the move and landed with both arms up and her feet in perfect alignment. Her teacher would have been proud. This time the hoots, whistles and screams of appreciation were deafening.

'Somersault with a one-and-a-half twist! Way to go, girl! Not bad for a Year 7 kid! I take it all back,' said Ben. Break looked sulky.

'Sorry to upstage you, gang leader, but it's good for you!' Charlie panted. 'Now, can we please talk about my dad?' They all walked up the steps and out into the sunlight. At the edge of the river there was a bench. While the others sat down, Charlie told them about finding her dad in the alleyway and the arrest.

'And you really don't think he did it?' asked Sanjay.

'No. I've gone over and over it. I trust him on this one. If he says he's straight, then he is. But something did happen to him that night and he wouldn't or couldn't tell me what it was. We need to speak to him to work out how he was framed and we need him out of that cell.'

'We...? OK, so what next?' said Ben.

Everyone turned to look at Break. 'Hey, stop looking at me! What are you suggesting, that we break him out of the police station?'

'What a great idea!' said Charlie.

'Oh yes. *Truly* great! Forty police officers against four school kids. That should be dead easy...' He paused for a moment and looked out over the grey, heaving mass of the river. 'But then...we could always talk to Prance!' Lance was Break's older brother, now at uni, studying and obsessed by drama and performing, hence the nickname. Break pulled back his hoodie and his eyes lit up. Charlie could see that under the messy mop of hair was a brain that was busy working the whole thing out. 'I'll just give him a ring. I've got an idea. If Prance is up for it, we'll have your dad out in a jiffy. And after that? Well, maybe we'll go hunting for some real criminals! It certainly beats spending our holidays playing video games. How about it?'

It was 8.00 am the following morning. According to Lance, first thing in the morning was the perfect time, right in the middle of shift changeover. The night-time drunks were being chucked out, couriers were delivering left, right and centre, and the front desk resembled a battle zone. The theory was good, but Lance still felt his Adam's apple bobbing up and down as he pushed open the swing door and entered the police station. Wearing a suit did not suit him and the greased-back hair, silk tie and brogues made him into an entirely different person. Which was the point of the whole exercise.

No going back now. He marched up to the front desk. 'Danny Cooper's brief. He rang me.'

The duty sergeant ignored him while he tried to sort out a particularly criminal Sudoku.

'Hello?' Lance helpfully rang the bell in case the policeman was deaf.

'You look too young to be earning so much

money!' was the man's only comment. The sergeant proceeded to pick his left ear, as if he might find an increased wage packet in there.

'Bit jealous, are we?'

'Not really. After all, our job is to keep the bad guys locked up but yours, it seems, *sir...*' and he emphasised the word *sir* as if it was a tropical disease, 'your job is to set them free.'

If only you knew! thought Lance, but smiled as the sergeant showed him which way to go. When he got to the door, the sergeant unlocked it and looked at his watch. 'Knock if you need someone. It won't be me. I'm off duty in a minute.' With that, he slammed the door and left them to it.

'Who the hell are you?' said Danny. He hadn't shaved in two days and looked as if police cells were definitely not good for his health.

'Your fairy godmother. The name's Lance. By the way, your daughter sends not only her love but me as well.'

Danny got up. 'Is she OK?' Like Charlie, Danny was the opposite of tall, which stood him in good stead in the breaking-and-entering business. He only came up to Lance's shoulders. Wiry was the adjective he preferred when describing himself.

'Listen. Don't worry. She believes you. We haven't got long.' Lance turned to his briefcase.

'I do hope this fits…' he muttered to himself. He turned round. 'Here we go!' Unrolled like a carpet in front of him was an entire three-piece suit. 'Luckily, there's a gang of male strippers, the Naughty Nudies, who rehearse in the same room as our am-dram lot. Managed to borrow it for the day, so long as I get it back in one piece.'

'What the…? You're not actually a solicitor, then? What on earth am I supposed to do with *that*?'

'Oh dear, Mr Cooper. You…put…it…on. The rest is called *acting*. You're going to do exactly what I just did: pretend to be a solicitor and walk straight out of here!'

The suit was all in one piece and Danny stepped into it while Lance stuck it back together with the Velcro fasteners. 'There are usually hoards of girls on stag nights who can't wait to rip this suit right off!'

Danny managed to smile at the thought.

'Last, but not least, stick these on.' In an instant Danny had a head of fine hair and a rather slick moustache. 'Right. Stand up straight. It's all in the posture and the angle of the chin. You have to walk like you own the place and they won't give you a second glance. Now, give me five minutes and then do what you've got to do. Here's a folder.

Hold it like you mean business. Good luck, and break a leg! Oh, by the way, your daughter retrieved this for you.' Lance threw a small packet on the bed. Danny couldn't believe it. Inside the wrapped-up cloth nestled a set of very interesting-looking keys. He felt like a little boy whose long-lost teddy bear has been miraculously recovered.

Lance knocked on the door while he motioned Danny to step to one side. The peep-hole swivelled open.

'Sorry about this. Caught short. Could you tell me where the, uh, bathroom is?'

The door clicked open and Danny flattened himself against the wall. The copper slammed the door shut and began to tell Lance where to go.

'Sorry again, can I interrupt? Directions are not my thing. Could you, would you be so kind as to...show me?' Lance had switched from super-cool solicitor to bumbling idiot in one second flat. The policeman stomped off ahead and after a few turns showed him the door. 'You're so kind. And if I could just trouble you for a few more seconds. The old car broke down and I had to take a bus in. They gave me this map...' Lance proceeded to unfold a huge map and dropped it to the floor. The policeman ground his teeth. Why should criminals get to do all the violence? Still, duffing up a solicitor wouldn't look good on his record.

While they were otherwise occupied, Danny set to work. The click of tumblers in a lock was like a symphony in which he knew every movement, and the finale was the satisfying click as the door swung open. Danny slipped his tools inside the folder and walked away from the cell. Lance had told him to hold his head high. 'You can get away with anything if you believe it. The human eye is trained to see the landscape. Fit into it, and you're invisible. Attitude is the best camouflage.' It was OK for him, and at least his costume fitted. Danny felt like he was wearing a tent. He tried to stop his hands shaking as he walked through a set of double doors and out into the lobby.

A different sergeant was now settled with a cup of tea behind the desk. This one was engrossed in the sports pages at the back of the paper. Only three paces away lay the street outside. Danny could almost smell the fresh air. Well, not so fresh actually. Most likely filled with diesel fumes and the stench of uncollected rubbish, but freedom nevertheless.

'Excuse me!' The sergeant looked up.

Danny almost had a heart attack. He stopped mid-stride and tried to hide the wobble in his voice. Was the copper at this moment pressing the panic button underneath his desk?

'Yes?' squeaked Danny.

The sergeant stared at him for a second as if he was trying to focus. Danny's legs had their own agenda, urging him to run and run *now*.

'You've dropped something.'

'Oh!' Danny looked down. His packet had slid out of the folder and onto the floor and the picklocks spilled out, gleaming. Every single one seemed to be screaming, 'Arrest that man!'

'Didn't know your lot had so many keys. I guess it's to lock up the secrets of how you get all those criminals off, eh?' sneered the sergeant.

'Yes! Ha! Ha!' laughed Danny, almost hysterically, as he scooped up the keys.

The sergeant wasn't going to let him go that easily. 'And if I were you, I'd use some of that dishonest money you earn and get yourself a suit that fits!' The sergeant chuckled to himself as if he'd just made up the funniest joke on record. Danny nodded, too scared to speak, and strode off through the doors.

Ten minutes later, Lance sauntered out and

passed by the desk sergeant who was now convinced there were far too many solicitors in the world and that a cull would be a great idea.

Having gone back to the cell after his loo visit, Lance had asked to be let out again within a few minutes, pointing out to the WPC who looked in through the door that poor Mr Cooper was exhausted by trying to prove his innocence and needed a little rest. The WPC saw a lump in the bed and let her tired eyes put two and two together and make five.

Within two hours, Danny was reunited with Charlie and settled into a tiny attic room at Lance's house-share. All the other students were away for the summer holiday so it made the perfect hideout. The rest of the gang assembled and after he's shared a few tearful hugs with Charlie, five expectant faces stared back at Danny as he told them about his meeting with Vince at the pub.

'So you reckon they spiked your drink?' asked Break.

'Well, I've never been drunk on Coca-Cola before. And why did it froth up so much?'

'They set you up, good and proper!' said Sanjay.

'Yeah. All for one little egg!'

'One very valuable egg, you mean,' chimed in

Charlie. 'Well, they will *not* get away with framing my dad. It's simple. We'll just have to find a way to prove it wasn't him.'

Everyone looked incredulous at first, then, one by one, began to nod. They were all in this together. There was no going back. It was time for revenge.

7. DOWN IN THE SEWERS

**Sunday 13 August, 2.45 am –
back to the present**

Break stared at the wall of water powering towards him, filling up the tunnel. It was almost fascinating. Part of him wanted simply to let go, give up, go with the flow. In a couple of seconds it would all be over and he'd be found a few days later, floating in the river, just another piece of rubbish filtered out through this great brick catacomb.

The ladder was still that bit too far in front of him. He felt like a tiny Smart car racing a whacking great diesel train to a level crossing. The advantage wasn't his. He pushed forwards against the water, which was now up to his shoulders. Only a few more metres. Maybe he could find a handhold somewhere? But the brick walls were smooth, worn down by years of liquid erosion. There was nothing to grip on to. He had no choice but to half-dive into the force of the flow with his hands flailing wildly under the surface as he tried to propel himself closer towards escape. His eyes were full of water. He couldn't see anything at all. He was going to have to go under again. He held his breath.

There! He caught hold of something. Could it be...? Yes! The bottom rung. There was an ominous creak as the current tried to drag him away, but the ladder held. He had a couple of seconds at most before the wave hit. An instinct for survival forced him upwards. His hands and legs went into automatic. He was on the third rung when the surge smashed into him. You wouldn't have thought it was water, the force of it; more like a concrete fist, punching and pummelling his body. He held on grimly as the current tried to bend his fingers off one by one. One last gasp of air and the flood sealed the tunnel like a plug. He existed only in a murky, dank underwater world and the roar of the water seemed to go on for ever.

How long could he hold his breath? He began to panic. There was no way out! Soon he'd have no choice but to open his mouth and breathe in death. A fragment of his mind reminded him of the geography lesson in which the teacher went on about the power of tides and how the worst thing you could do was fight the current. Oh yeah? His feet found the bottom rungs and his hand kept going.

Come on, Break! Don't be so pathetic! He felt like a sponge soaking up the water until he was heavier than stone. Easy to sink down...another rung...there! His head was above water. He opened his mouth and sucked in the stale air as if it was the perfume of the gods. He was alive! The rest of his body slipped out like a snail from its shell, until all that was left was the dark underground river rushing below his feet and slowly welling up the ladder. He dragged himself up. The ladder had to go somewhere, though in the pitch dark, he wondered if this was true.

His head bumped. Metal. That was it! Time to push. He was so tired, though, and it felt like the grate was rusted shut. He wanted to scream, but what story could he tell anyone who came along? No, he was on his own with this one. If he had no idea where he was, neither would the others. There was a screech and the grate finally shifted.

He poked his head out and there, in front of him, was a sight that made a smile break out over his mud-stained face: Big Ben's clock face gleaming down like a friendly full moon as it chimed 3.00 am. He slithered out and flopped onto the pavement, hoping no one was there to see this strange fish emerge from the shadows.

Unbelievably, apart from his sore shoulders, he seemed all in one piece. He felt in his pockets. Wallet, mobile, keys, memory stick (empty) and iPod. The phone was dead, but the iPod lit up as if to say that severe underground flooding was no problem, man. Break was too tired to be glad as he dripped his way home. All this, and it wasn't even him that had the information. Worse, he was without wheels. The whole concept of walking was too alien; he felt like a sailor on dry land.

Still, they'd done it. At least he hoped that the gang had got away. With his mobile dead as a dodo, he had no idea. As he hugged the edges of alleys and did his best to avoid CCTV, his mind went back to the first few days after Danny was freed. The police had been all over Charlie's house – but who would ever suspect her? They assumed that the unknown gang had broken Danny out, and the desk sergeant had been given a nice, long stint on traffic duty. Meanwhile, Danny was still a prisoner at Lance's place, unable to leave for fear of being caught, but at least he was among friends.

As for Vince, it was him who'd set Charlie's dad up. No doubt about that. And it was Vince who had the egg. Danny knew how the man operated. No mobiles, no emails, so there was nothing for Sanjay to hack into. Danny put the word around a few of his mates and it turned out there was going to be a secret auction. But the trickle of information dried up. Sanjay finally had a breakthrough: he got into the Companies House website and found all the companies that Vince and his family owned. It was a web as good as any spider's, with Vince hiding behind shell companies and holding false businesses as far away as Belize and the Cayman Islands. But finally Sanjay managed to get behind all the masks to one company, one building.

Danny had hoped it was that simple. Break in, get the egg back to the owners and prove his innocence. But Vince wasn't stupid. The only thing the building held in its dark core was pictures. The actual egg was too well hidden. The way Danny found that out was a certain Piggy who couldn't help squealing to one of his mates in the pub one night after a beer too many. That was the problem with brainless bodyguards. They might be good at the old Punch and Judy, but keeping a secret? That was another matter. And after a few too many you have to show off a bit, don't you? What mattered is that they had a target and that was the first step.

Danny couldn't risk being seen, and at first he was against the idea of kids breaking and entering, but Charlie gave him a good bit of lip. What was the alternative, anyway? Wait for the police to come and find him again while Vince got clean away with it? Forget it.

Break was tired and the thought of a nice warm bed hovered in front of him as he pushed the key quietly into the lock and stood in the hallway listening out for his mother. It was one thing taking on a criminal mastermind, but his mum was in another league altogether. He stripped off in the dark bathroom and shoved his clothes into the wash. Just as he was tiptoeing down the corridor in a clean T-shirt and boxers, the lights flicked on.

'I never knew that it rained inside the house, Arthur Collins!' His mother stood there with her hands on her hips and a frown very firmly planted on her face.

Not good. If she was using his second name the signs were very bad indeed.

'Umm.'

'Don't you *Umm* me! It's the middle of the night. I've just delivered twins at the hospital and they showed their gratitude by screaming even louder than their mother and being helpfully covered in bits of stuff I don't even want to tell you about...And now I have to deal with this soaking-wet teenager!'

'Not my fault. It was a...taxi, driving too fast and hit a big puddle, nearly knocked me off my board and then...' Break was thinking on his feet, '...drove over it. Trashed. Kaput.'

'Do you want to know something about mothers? They can tell when their beloved children are lying their soaking-wet socks off! Now go to bed, and we can discuss the appropriate punishment in the morning.' She looked at her watch. 'Which isn't even that far away now, it's so late!' His hassled mother then grabbed him and planted a kiss on his forehead as if to say that he might be bad, but she'd just about put up with him.

8. COMPUTER SECRETS

Sunday 13 August, 10.00 am – next morning

The next morning, Break's mother left him a note on the breakfast table, offering him the chance to take on hoovering, washing up and general cleaning duties for the next four weeks. Either that, or no allowance for two months. The choice was pretty obvious, but breakfast did not go with a swing, and his whole body ached. As soon as he was a bit more conscious, and with the kitchen presentable, he cursed his dead mobile and rang Sanjay on the house phone.

An hour later, he sat nursing a cup of sweet, milky tea in the attic room at Lance's.

'Let's see what you've got, then,' Break said to

San, who loaded the memory stick into the back of his borrowed laptop.

'What, no congratulations on our incredibly daring raid?'

'Fine. I'll say well done when you burst into applause as I tell you how I not only did the finest skate stunt of the twenty-first century, but then managed to take on a monster flood in the confines of this city's fetid sewers and survived to tell the tale!'

'Boys!' Charlie butted in. 'As far as I know, it's not a competition, so quit with the macho thing, eh? We all worked the plan to a tee and got what we came for, so stop bickering! Anyhow, you didn't have the police following your every move, unlike me – as if I was stupid enough to lead them to my dad!' Danny winked at his daughter and looked so proud he could almost burst.

Break muttered to himself while Ben winked at Charlie.

San tapped away at the keys for a couple of minutes. 'Ooh. Now *that* is a lovely bit of code. Self-executing and even with digital rights management. Impressive…almost!'

'Could you talk in a language we understand for a change?' complained Break.

'Yeah, yeah. Just wait a mo'… Here we are!' The

egg flashed up on the screen. Only this time it was a slideshow of images in close up, showing the detailed enamel leaves with pearl flowers and the green-gold cabriolet legs. Each picture had a hand with a newspaper held out towards the camera, the date underlined to show it was taken after the egg had been stolen.

'What a beauty!' whispered Danny.

'That's what I thought!' answered San. 'I mean, here you have a program that can only be copied onto single disks. The CDs will play once, then the code turns them to gibberish. Someone clever put this together, but they didn't reckon on the talents of a thirteen-year-old computer geek!'

Everyone groaned.

'So this is what we broke in for? Some worthless digital pictures?' complained Ben and sucked his teeth as if the whole thing was a waste of time.

'Not so fast, my friends. There's a letter, too.' The text scrolled up on screen. An invitation to a viewing where prospective buyers could not only see the egg but also meet with an expert, who would be brought in to verify that this was indeed what it purported to be.

'The sale of the century!' said Danny.

'And one of us has to be there.' Break frowned in concentration.

'Thing is, there're only a few buyers who would risk this and who would be rich enough to bid. They're known faces, and each of them will already have a copy of this disk,' Danny carried on. 'So we're stuck. Unless...'

'What?' said Break.

'Have you wondered why I know so much about these eggs?'

'That's like asking me why I can name every type of board, truck and wheel from a distance of twenty paces. If you're in the game, you need to know the pieces you play with.'

'Exactly. I always prided myself on being a cultural thief. When you're out to steal a bit of history it would be common not to know what you're sticking in the bag.' Danny stood up and went to the window to look out on the street. 'Mind if I have a fag?'

'Yes!' said Charlie and stared at him until he put the packet back in his pocket.

'When Vince stuck that photo in front of me at the pub, I wondered if he'd been spying on me as I'd heard all about that egg from one of the lags in prison, an old guy by the name of Theodore Perchin...' He paused as if the name meant something. A bunch of blank faces looked back at him. 'Oh well, they don't teach you much in school these days... Thing is, the guy was a forger. In fact, a very good one, until he got caught. The name rang a bell with me and I had a chat with him out in the yard one day. When I found out I was talking to the great-grandson of Michael Perchin himself, I was dumbfounded, I tell you!' Danny pronounced the name as Mick-ay-ell.

'Who?' said Ben.

'Give me a chance! If you go back to the late nineteenth century, Peter Carl Fabergé hired a young Russian goldsmith by the name of Michael Evlampievich Perchin to research the ancient and lost techniques of goldsmithing. Perchin was a genius who did the actual work and his boss was the marketing man who came up with the idea of the ever-more extravagant Easter-egg gifts for the Tsar and the Empress. She was in love with the colour pink and had pink lilies of the valley all over her apartments. This egg was the perfect gift.

'So, we're wandering round the yard and this old guy with a beard and an accent is telling me the story. Poor guy, he was the black sheep of the family – three generations of goldsmithing, and he had the bright idea of becoming the first Perchin forger, copying old Fabergé pieces and selling them privately to obsessive collectors. Unfortunately, one of them had a piece analysed and found that the enamel had originated not in nineteenth-century Russia, but in a twenty-first-century art shop. So that's why he was paying a visit to the local HMP. He left shortly after I got there – open prison, I think. Even allowed him his own workshop, so he could make new pieces, but this time, properly dated and signed.'

Danny sighed. 'There's one more thing. And I can't tell if the guy was spinning me a tale or not. The night before he left, Theodore came to my cell during recreation. He wanted to tell me about the love of his great-grandfather's life. I tried to look as bored as I could, but the old man was lonely, so I thought I'd humour him. He told me that his great-grandfather had met the Empress several times when the eggs were presented to the family. She was fascinated by the inner workings and secret compartments that made the eggs more than what they seemed. She even invited him to her apartments to explain how the eggs were made. Family legend had it that although he was a humble goldsmith, he fell in love with the great woman but could never declare it. Instead, it was said that one of the eggs held a message for her, a hidden treasure that expressed his true feelings in the only way he knew how – through a jewel...'

A hush fell over the attic room.

'And was it ever found?' said Lance.

'That's the point. Never. All that survived was the story. But when Vince showed me the photo, I just wondered if legend could come to life. If any egg had a secret, it would be the one Perchin dedicated to the Empress.'

Danny continued, 'And I guess there's only one way to find out. I've been accused of stealing the egg once already. We might as well steal it for real!'

9. THE EXPERT

Charlie checked on her mum, left her a cup of tea, picked up her board and locked the door. She looked down the road. The same two plain-clothes men in the same unmarked Ford sat there looking bored out of their minds. She was tempted to walk over and ask if they wanted to use her loo. Still, if they had nothing better to do, they were welcome to follow her. She put her board to the ground and pushed off. No one denied Break was best, but in terms of speed, she could easily keep up. She leapt over kerbs and even took on a few benches, giving the odd 50-50 grind just to show she wasn't a total beginner.

They'd arranged to meet at Ben's house. The

police were hardly likely to suspect a couple of twin toddlers and a baby.

'Hello Mrs O,' she said, as Ben's harassed-looking mother opened the door.

'Nice to see you, Charlotte! Here, have baby Thomas!' Ben's mother handed the bundle over while Charlie stowed her board. Mrs Olatunji was one of the few people who called her by her full name and got away with it. From inside came the smell of something good.

'Got us some chicken an' rice on the go for an early lunch if you're not rushing off?' Charlie smiled and made silly noises at the tiny face that stared up at her as she carried Ben's baby brother into the living room. 'I never say no to your cooking, Mrs O!'

Ben's mother smiled and vanished into the kitchen.

Break, San and Ben were already there. Break was not only on the floor playing with the three-year-old twins, but smiling his head off. Even San was doing his famous farmyard animal impressions.

'Hi Charlie.' Ben did his best to look disinterested.

'Full house?' Thomas had managed to get hold of Charlie's little finger and now gripped it as if he was hanging on for dear life.

'Yeah. Can't wait to get out of here. If it ain't the baby puking all over my shoulder as I try to burp him, it's the twins doing tantrums in sequence!'

'Your poor mother!' said Charlie.

'It's me you should be feeling sorry for, girl!'

'Stop whining, Ben! That's what babies and toddlers do. Isn't it, you wuvly, bubbly, jubbly thing!' she cooed as the baby's face lit up.

Ben frowned but his sulkiness vanished as his mother brought in a tray of chicken wings and bowls of steaming rice.

'You all too thin!' said Mrs Olatunji. She came over and pinched Charlie's arm. 'Girl – you made of bone, I swear! Now eat up!' Charlie delivered Thomas back into his mother's arms.

The gang needed no convincing and tucked in. The spicy chicken was delicious, crispy and greasy. Charlie would have to get the recipe for her dad. This would keep a load of gas-platform workers going in the North Sea, no problem.

'I read about your father...' said Ben's mother. 'Now the papers sound as if they made up their minds. But, when I saw him after all his trouble, I knew he was a changed man!' She put her hand on Charlie's arm and held it there. 'I know he's innocent, girl, I really do.' She turned away and Charlie did her best not to cry.

As the plates were cleared away, Mrs Olatunji turned to her son. 'Now, don't you be doing anything to get yourself in trouble, huh?'

Ben stayed silent and everyone suddenly found the wallpaper very interesting.

Twenty minutes later and half a mile away, the gang swept into one of their favourite outdoor spots. It was a square, surrounded by trees, plenty of tarmac and the odd obstacle. As skaters, they were obsessed with obstacles of any sort. How could you leap/slidealong/grind/balance and generally find interesting ways to cross from one side to another? It was like three-dimensional chess but with faster moves and the odd spark.

'How is he?' asked Charlie.

'Lance tells me he's feeling cooped up in there, pacing up and down all day,' said Break. 'The sooner we get moving, the sooner we can prove he's innocent.'

'Yeah, and the sooner we get that lot off our backs.' Charlie flicked her eyes backwards. The Ford with tinted windows was too obvious.

'Teenagers on skateboards? Hardly looks like a conspiracy!' smiled Ben.

There was a rectangular concrete block about half a metre high that was sadly what the local council thought of as street furniture. But they weren't complaining. Break had managed to borrow a board from his dad, an 'old school' skater who now managed the park under the motorway flyover. After ollieing onto the block and manualling off the edge in a perfect wheelie a few times, he slowed down and managed a nice K-grind, balancing on the front of the board as his truck ground along the edge.

'Nice one!' said Ben, then flipped his board so that the nose slid along the edge. 'A couple more nose-blunts and I'll have to get a new deck!'

A few other skaters had arrived and soon they were taking turns.

San ignored everyone, sitting on his old and rather unfashionable board and poking a stylus at his PDA screen. He'd seen all the tricks before.

Charlie pushed the board away from her and as it trundled off, she ran at it, cartwheeling until her hands were on the board and she turned into a speeding handstand. She carried on the cartwheel until the board was above her head and then gave a little bow.

'Might as well give them a good show!'

San looked up. 'They think I'm playing video

games, but I've just gained access to Piggy's email system. Piggy, you are the weakest link! He's doing as his boss has told him, sorting out the experts. Thing is, there's only three people in the world who have enough knowledge. The first one works for the guy who owned the eggs in the first place. The second is straight as an arrow and doesn't speak English, but the third, well...third time lucky, as they say!' A wicked grin crossed Sanjay's face.

'I don't get it,' said Charlie.

'You don't, but Break's older brother certainly will.'

'You're joking!' said Ben, putting his board down and staring at the screen.

'Not really. I've just hijacked the guy's contact details and forwarded his website. Once Lance has done a little photo session for us I'll upload the pictures and hey presto – your nineteen-year-old brother, courtesy of an extreme makeover from the theatrical make-up department, will hopefully be none other than Vladimir Vinokurov, expert in pre-revolutionary Russian jewellery and crooked as a silver pin.'

'Let's have a look at the guy he's going to impersonate!' said Break. The face that stared up from the tiny screen had a goatee, little glasses and slicked-back grey hair. Somehow, the eyes managed to convey both extreme intelligence and absolute cunning at the same time. Break frowned. 'If my brother can become this little crook, I'll give him an Oscar myself!'

'But how is that going to help?' asked Charlie. 'It's one thing for Lance to enter a police station and break my dad out, but you're not expecting him to walk off with the egg, are you? Vince's gang don't use pea-shooters and spud-guns, you know.'

San frowned. 'No, nicking the egg would be a problem, I admit. Lance just needs access and a few private moments alone with the egg. That's all. But it's time for us to pay a visit to Danny Cooper's new friend!' San switched off his PDA.

By now, the square was growing busy. A couple of in-line bladers were practising fakie jumps, zooming backwards, jumping and twisting round in 360s and 540s. Some older teenagers had commandeered the concrete block, shredding it with a variety of aerial tricks. Various office workers lounged on the grass bed, smoking cigarettes, having important conversations on their mobiles and eating takeaway sandwiches. The crowd made perfect cover.

Ben pulled out an old hoodie and as he walked away from the car and among the various groups, he put it on and pulled up the hood. A few seconds later, the gang split in four directions and headed away from the square.

Ben was the first to sprint off, straight towards the watching policemen. Cars were one of his favourite bits of urban landscape. There was so much you could do with them. But this move was his favourite and should certainly get a response. All the training he did at his mum's gym was about to pay off. He leapt onto the boot in one swift movement, put both hands on the roof and forward-rolled over the top and down the front, rocking the car as he took off from the bonnet, and landed still in full sprint.

Two car doors swung open. 'Oi! You little git!' But a pair of waddling overweight officers, whose training was somewhere distant in the mists of time, were no competition for a free-runner at the top of his game. The dead end straight ahead was perfect. The cops slowed, thinking how delightful it would be to handcuff the annoying tearaway and do him for damaging police property. Their faces fell as Ben bounced off the wall with one leg, his hands grabbing the ledge three metres up. He hauled himself up, turned to wave goodbye to his pursuers stuck in the alley below, and leapt down to continue his journey to the rendezvous.

When the officers returned to their car, not only were the others long gone, but their four tyres were mysteriously as flat as pancakes. One of them kicked the door in frustration. Not a good idea. He screamed as his big toe protested in agony and the remaining skaters in the square nearly wet themselves with laughter.

Half an hour and a bus ride later, the gang pressed a buzzer on a door in a cobbled street filled with warehouses. It seemed to be one of the few such places in the city that hadn't yet been done up into too-expensive apartments. Charlie could smell leather and spices, and had the sense that work was going on behind shuttered windows.

The door opened and an old man stood in front of them. He was so tall they all looked up, even Ben. The glasses were pebbled, and the hair and thin beard that covered his chin a uniform grey.

'Yes?' barked the man, staring at them suspiciously.

Charlie stepped forward. 'I'm Danny Cooper's daughter.'

'And I'm ze Michael Perchin's great-grandson!' said the man in a thick Russian accent. 'But as I don't know who you are talking about, goodbye!' He turned and began to close the door.

'No, wait!' Charlie had to think quickly. 'Your great-grandfather was in love with Alexandra Fedorovna, Empress of Russia!'

The man's jaw dropped. 'You...how...?' He squinted up and down the street and then pulled the door open wider. 'Quick. In, now, and up ze stairs, ze door on ze right.' He rolled his r's as he spoke.

The gang ran up the stairs and walked into the apartment. The old man shuffled up behind them and locked and chained the door. The room was enormous, with central iron pillars holding up the roof and floor-to-ceiling windows. Along one side of the wall ran a huge workbench covered in tools, magnifying glasses and – Charlie could see as the light streamed in – coils of gold wire, hoops, half-set rings and boxes filled with glittering stones.

'Mostly costume jewellery – paste and glass, I'm afraid. Honest commissions don't pay nearly enough and my main job is to copy classic pieces for ze museum shops.' The man shook his head. 'It is quite humbling but I have learnt my lesson...'

He walked to the corner of the room where an old Belfast sink sat on some very rickety wooden legs and an improvised worktop held a brown-stained kettle. 'Do the children these days drink tea?' Without waiting for an answer, he carried on. 'I make it Russian style, with lemon. Now sit, *sit!*' He cleared space from an enormous sagging sofa that took up the middle of the room.

Each of the gang was presented with a glass cup and saucer. A little wedge of lemon floated in the hot tea and a bowl of sugar was passed round.

'Now. Tell me. Zis Danny Cooper. I have heard such name before, no?'

'He was in jail with you!'

'Ah yes, now I remember, ze great safe-breaker. A most marvellous man!' Theodore smiled. 'And now, I read in papers he has stolen my great-grandfazer's egg, yes? I vould rather he had it zan some museum.'

'That's the thing, Mr Perchin,' said Charlie. 'He didn't steal it, but he knows who did. We want you to help prove he's innocent.'

'A thief who does not steal asks help from a forger who no longer forges. Zis vill be interesting indeed. I read ze story told by ze papers. Did you free him from ze police station?' The shrewd eyes stared at them one by one.

Break spoke up. 'It was my plan, helped by my older brother who acted the solicitor.'

The jeweller clapped his hands in glee. 'You are

my kind of people. My ancestor, viz his secrets and most intricate plans, vould have much love for you!'

As they sipped their surprisingly aromatic tea, Charlie explained what they wanted him to do.

'Oh. It is an honour to be asked. But you say I have only ten days to complete zis task!' Theodore ran his hand through his grey hair. 'Such vork, it is…impossible.'

Charlie was close to tears. 'You're our last chance, Mr Perchin. We know you can do it and I have to save my father.'

'Ah! You are a noble child. The Empress vould have been most impressed by your convictions! I am svayed by your tears, now put zem avay and let us talk furzer!'

He led them over to the workbench and after half an hour of discussing ways to cut corners without giving the game away, the jeweller ushered them out of his front door.

'I must vork on zis, how you say, twenty-four seven. But I zink old Michael himself vill be guiding my hands. Do not phone me. When I am ready, I vill send you a signal through ze evening paper. It vill be addressed to Lily. Zen you vill know!' There was a gleam in his eye as he shut the door. The deal was done, but would it work?

10. TWO FAKES

**Wednesday 23 August, 10.45 pm –
eight days later**

'We could really do with Charlie right now!'
whispered San.

They crouched in the shadows behind some
overflowing rubbish bins. The warehouse stood
in front of them and the street was eerily quiet
apart from the faint buzz of the streetlamps and
the far-off hum of traffic. A single light bulb
blazed through the grimy windows.

'No way. Remember what I said?' Break
answered. 'We have to leave her out of it.
Anyhow, we're two days early, it's late and once
Piggy's left the building, it'll be ours for the
night!'

Vince was good on the strategy. San would give

him that. The buyers were assembling from all over the world. But all they knew was that it would be somewhere in the city. Two hours before the viewing, each would receive a text message telling them the location. Piggy's suit trousers now had a tiny self-adhesive tracking device dropped into the turn-ups – courtesy of a drunken moment with Prance in a pub when Break's older brother decided his shoelaces needed tying up.

A simple bit of GPS tracking and San could map out Piggy's every movement. And part of a heavy's job is to scope out suitable spots for skulduggery. All San and Break had to do was play 'follow my leader'.

Vince's sense of humour was on form as ever. He'd recently knocked off a huge consignment of chocolate eggs and they were being stored here until the right time of year. There wasn't much of a profit margin in foil-wrapped confectionery, but an egg of a different sort...that was another matter entirely.

The light that shone over the alley was suddenly switched off. Break put a finger to his lips.

The doors of the warehouse slid shut and Piggy started towards the car. He was in the middle of lovingly unwrapping a chocolate egg and was about to take a huge, yummy bite when…

San made the mistake of leaning back. A rubbish bag split open and the contents spilled all over him.

'What's going on, eh?' said Piggy, dropping the egg as he advanced down the alley.

Break and San froze. They weren't get-away artists like Ben and Charlie, and the muscles that threatened to burst from Piggy's suit were aching to be used.

'Come on, then! If there's someone in there, I'd like them to meet my two friends: Fist One and Fist Two. Interrupting my snack was the last mistake you'll ever make!' Piggy cracked his knuckles to make his point.

They were both about to stand up when a mangy tabby cat ran out from behind them. San almost punched the air in joy.

The effect on Piggy was remarkable as the cat rubbed round his legs.

''Ello darlin'! Oh, they don't feed you proper, do they? How about you and me go and get you a bit of Whiskas Delight? For a second there, I thought you were trouble, but you're no trouble at all.' Piggy softened all over as he picked up the purring cat, stuck him in his car and drove off.

'That was close! Remind me to donate my allowance to the next cat-rescue shop we come across,' said Break, standing up and stretching his legs. The coast was clear.

After climbing up a drainpipe, Break found a loose skylight.

'Oi!' hissed Sanjay. 'Have you got all my stuff?'

'Stop worrying. It'll kill you one day! Now keep a lookout and fire up your screen.' Break clambered in through the window and vanished while San peered up the alleyway.

Five minutes later, San heard Break on his earpiece.

'Here it is. Where do you want me to place the cameras?'

'As high up as possible, and train them down on the centre.' The cameras were already on and with Break's torch illuminating the space, San's touch screen came to life. As Break climbed up the pallets that edged the room, he placed each camera pointing inwards until San had a complete three-hundred-and-sixty-degree view of the interior. 'We have visual. Time to get out, Break!' San used his remote to switch off the cameras and preserve battery power. He breathed a sigh of relief when the dark figure slipped out of the skylight and slid down the drainpipe. Setup was complete. It was up to Theodore now.

Two days later, Charlie crouched by the bathroom sink with her mobile. It didn't seem fair. 'But I could lose them, easily!'

'No,' said Break, 'it's too dangerous.' Ever since the incident in the square, surveillance at Charlie's house had been increased. The officers had tried it on the following day, but how could they prove that some boy or girl wearing a hoodie had been one of her gang? She told them to show her some evidence and shut the door in their faces with a satisfying slam.

'Look. We'll ring you when the meeting's over, OK? There's a lot to do. Gotta go.' Break hung up and Charlie screwed up her face, trying not to cry. It was her *dad*! She should be there, but now she was just like him – trapped, and to top it all in her own home. At least with the pay-as-you-go mobile that San had lent her and the trick of running water from the tap while she spoke, she was safe from being overheard.

Break picked up the paper and reread the advert in the lonely hearts column, just to make sure.

A weariness comes from those dreamers,
dew-dabbled, the lily and rose;
Ah, dream not of them, my beloved,
the flame of the meteor that goes.
W.B. Yeats. Call round tonight.

Whoever this Yeats guy was, he sure knew how to write. Break felt the hairs on the back of his neck rise up. If Theodore pulled it off, they were in with a chance. He texted San, Ben and Lance and set off towards the workshop.

The figure that greeted him at the door looked a little bit older and greyer. But the smile on his face said it all.

'Quick. You come now. Your comrades are here before you!' Theodore almost pushed him up the stairs. The others were sitting on the sofa. Break's eyes strayed towards the workbench. There was something there, covered in a silk cloth. As ever, Theodore would not be rushed. The making of tea was a necessary ritual. 'As zey say in my country, a guest in ze house is God in ze home!' He passed around the cups and some homemade hazelnut biscuits.

'Ha! I pick zeeze nuts fresh from your parks. You like?' Four heads nodded as they tucked in. 'All zis free food and you silly British go to supermarket instead!'

Break opened his mouth to speak but Theodore put his hand up.

'Yes. I know vat you come for. I have vorked many late nights and seen many dawns since you vere last here. And...such a thing I have made!' He walked to his workbench and lifted the cloth.

'Why, it's...'

'Beautiful. Yes! I know. I vill not hide my craftsmanship! Come, look and touch!' He cradled the replica of the Lilies of the Valley egg as if it were a newborn child. 'And *voilà*, I press down ze crown so and see vot happens!' It was just like the photos. The egg opened out and the three miniature portraits of the Tsar and two of his children unfolded like flower petals.

'To most eyes, it vill pass, although ze pearls are not real and ze gold is...vell, your expert vill help on zis matter, no?'

Break stared at his older brother. Lance was trying to shrink into the sofa. 'I'm not too sure about all this!'

'Come on, Prance. You were born for this part. Theodore here can work on your accent!'

'Why can't we just let the police round them up now we know where they're going to be?'

'Listen!' said Break. 'It's called revenge. They

nearly did for Charlie's dad. It's time to turn the tables. Who wants the police to get all the glory in any case? They've never done us any favours! Anyhow, I thought you enjoyed all this dressing-up stuff!'

Prance scowled but couldn't think of any other excuse.

They passed the egg round until Sanjay had it in his hands. It was a masterpiece. The detail was incredible.

'I have also hidden a little surprise for our friends in zere and checked it vorks viz ze remote control. Your friend Sanjay is very clever for his age!'

Sanjay smiled. 'And you're sure they won't find it?'

'It vould dishonour my great-grandfazer's name if I could not do vot you have asked. Trust me, zey vill not!'

Sanjay nodded. He couldn't wait for the look on Vince's face. He put the egg back onto the workbench. He reckoned that even the Empress would have been fooled.

The doorbell went. Theodore nearly jumped as he ran to the egg and hid it in one of the many workbench drawers.

'Calm down, Mr Perchin!' said Break. 'It's one of Prance's fellow students come to improve his image with a bit of cosmetic surgery.'

Theodore let Break get the door and a few seconds later he returned with a girl about Prance's age, with blond hair and wearing no make-up at all.

'Hello!' she said brightly. As the assembled gang turned to stare, they couldn't decide which was more beautiful, the egg or her.

'I've come to help Lance with his Chekhov audition. By the time I've finished with him, he should look the part!' she gushed. 'And you must be Mr Perchin, part-time voice coach!' She came up to Theodore and pumped his hand vigorously up and down. When she finally let go, he stared at his mangled fingers for a second until he realised that his new guest would need liquid refreshment. But before he could turn away to the kettle, the girl was already issuing orders:

'Theodore – do you mind if I call you that? – can you turn on the overhead light, and Lance, you need to grab a stool and sit directly under it. That way we can see where the shadows fall on your face and accentuate them.'

'Yes, Enid,' answered Lance.

Break mouthed the word *Enid* at Lance with a question mark at the end. Lance shrugged his shoulders as if to say, how should I know why her parents inflicted that name on her?

'Now, you've told the director that you really are in your late forties. Ha! Ha! Great idea. By the time I'm done, you will be. Break, do you have that picture for me?'

Break dumbly handed over an A4 print-out of the real Victor.

'Hmm…yes, I can see the challenge. He looks a shifty sort of fellow! You tell me – what's the first step before I set to work on you?' Break held up a mirror so that Lance could see his face.

'Foundation, of course. You can't do anything without it.'

'Well done. They're training you well.'

While Lance covered his face and neck, the girl carried on her lecture. 'The trick is to use the light to find your natural lines, and then I can create wrinkles with an eyebrow pencil. I'll highlight the sunken areas around your eyes and finish with your hands.'

Underneath the light, Lance was growing older far more quickly than nature intended. A spray-on dye combed through his hair gave him the necessary grey streaks, and once the make-up was complete it was time for finishing touches. Enid applied some spirit gum to Lance's chin and pressed on the instant goatee. A pair of small glasses completed the transformation.

Lance stood up with a slight stoop. 'Zis vill not be easy for me, you know!'

Theodore clapped his hands together. 'Yes! You listen vell to my accent. Very good. Very good indeed!'

The young actor hobbled around the room as if the legendary Russian winters had frozen his bones.

Enid looked at her creation and gave a beaming smile. All five males in the room sighed. 'Not bad. It will do.' She took a quick slurp of tea, plucked her mobile from her bag and speed-dialled a number. 'Yes. No. Be there in a jiffy, darling!' She snapped the phone shut and blew a kiss at Lance. 'Got to go. Video shoot in need of my services. Great pay and one more blow to student debt. Toodle-oo!' Then she was out of the door like a whirlwind.

Ben looked depressed as San nudged him in the ribs.

'She's well out of your league and age range, boy!' he muttered.

'Are ve ready?' said Lance.

'You're not supposed to give credit to older brothers under any circumstances, but in this case, you're hired!' said Break. 'Let's just hope we don't end up with egg all over our faces!'

11. VERIFICATION

Friday 25 August, 7.30 pm – that evening

'Let's avoid the rubbish bins this time, eh?' said Break as he pulled up on his board. The warehouse was three blocks away and they had about fifteen minutes.

'We need to be within two hundred metres to get a decent picture and make sure we can keep radio contact with your brother. The more walls the signal has to go through, the weaker it gets,' San frowned.

'How about a fire escape?' suggested Ben.

'Good one, Dread! We'll get round the back of the next-door building. Close enough if Lance is in trouble, but not for Vince's goons to eyeball us.'

The three of them wheeled off towards their destination.

'Hey!' a voice called out to them.

'What are you doing here? You want to spoil the whole thing?' Break was furious. This wasn't part of the plan.

'You know, Break, it's time to stop treating me like a kid sister!' said Charlie as she ran up to them, her board slung across her shoulder bag.

'Yeah, but only a kid sister would be stupid enough to bring half the police force along for the ride!' countered Break.

'Thanks, Break. I was given these legs for a reason, you know! I ducked into the local shopping centre and out through the emergency exit. As far as I know, at this moment, that "half-a-police-force" are stuck in the pound shop buying counterfeit bottles of shampoo!'

'*Touché!*' said Break and smiled. 'Come on then, we'll be late!'

Five minutes later and after lifting up the bent corrugated sheeting that was what passed for security, they were in a weed-strewn concrete patch at the back of yet another abandoned warehouse.

'Do you think that shopping trolleys are like migrating species?' said Ben, pointing out a particularly rusty example. 'I swear, if you put down a camera long enough you'd see them mating and making baby trolleys!' Everyone laughed.

'How's your dad doing?' asked Break.

'Not so good,' said Charlie. 'I'm managing to bring him food and stuff as Lance hasn't quite worked out the cooking thing yet. But he misses home and if this doesn't get sorted soon, he's out of a job and back where he started.' Charlie looked down. This was the reason why she was here. At least she felt she was doing something. And being cooped up in the house with Mum stuck in front of her endless musicals was no fun at all.

'Hey,' said Break. 'Sorry about earlier. Good to have you on board.' Charlie smiled and San fired up his PDA.

Even at this distance, they could feel the tension. There was Vince, pacing up and down, in and out of the shadow of the single light bulb. Piggy guarded the egg and Dirk controlled the door. As far as San could make out, there were four buyers – three in suits and one in flowing Arabic robes, all men. It was eerie, watching the screen. There was no sound, so the actions seemed exaggerated, as if they were watching an old silent movie. The buyers milled round the egg, the glint in their eyes reflecting their greed.

Piggy made sure they didn't get too close and played the menacing thug to perfection.

One of the buyers looked at his watch, as if to signify that important people such as him should not be kept waiting. Right on cue, Vince looked up as the door opened and in came the expert.

The watching gang were transfixed. This was the moment. If a hair was out of place or something smelt wrong, the cameras would reveal it. But all they saw was the buyers' looks of appraisal. They studied the new figure as if he was also for sale, and nothing in his features, from small goatee to greying hair, disappointed them. The figure limped forward to shake Vince's hand and present his card.

'Here is my card! Vladimir Vinokurov at your service!' Lance gave his most polished smile as the sweat broke out on his upper lip.

'Yeah, at my service for a whacking great big wodge of money, you mean!' snarled Vince quietly enough for the buyers not to hear.

'A small recompense for my expertise!' Lance fluttered his hands to indicate that talk of such things was beneath him. He then turned to the centre of the room and put out his arms as if greeting a long-lost love. 'Ah! The Lilies of the Valley egg. I vould never have thought to see such a thing in my life!' He moved towards the egg, pushing a bemused Piggy aside. In one movement he put his briefcase on the floor and picked up the egg, then delicately traced the pink enamel with his fingers.

Back at the fire escape, Charlie blurted out, 'He's not going to make the switch now?'

'Charlie. Shut. Up!' said San. 'Think about it. Everyone's watching. Why do you think we've got the cameras? This is the moment when a fake verifies the real thing.'

'How could anyvun but ze great Mick-ay-ell Perchin make such a translucent rose enamel!' Lance held the egg up to the light. 'See how it shines, and ze striations, ze pattern of vaves called "guilloche" inscribed under ze surface!' He had them now. The buyers were like little boys, ears soaking up facts like sponges. 'And to top it all, ze imperial crown in rose diamonds and cabochon rubies. Twist ze pearl at ze top, like so, and...'

A collective sigh went up among the small crowd. Every one of them knew what to expect, but to see that magical inner machinery work so smoothly after over one hundred years almost brought tears to their eyes.

With a flourish, Lance pulled out a small jeweller's magnifying glass and bent his eye towards the pictures. 'It is not enough zat ze portraits are a credit to ze miniaturist's art, but zeir frames of rose diamonds and ze date of 5 April 1898 engraved on the back completes my examination!' Lance gently placed the egg back on the stand, almost regretfully.

'For many years I have studied zese artefacts from ze workshop of Carl Fabergé. Whoever buys today is purchasing history!' He gave a little bow and the audience almost burst into applause, before the bemused buyers remembered they were here strictly illegally and that it was time to get down to business.

Vince came over immediately and put his arm around Lance's shoulders and held him so tightly it hurt. 'Thank you, Mr Vinokurov. Your expertise shines through. The quoted fee was worth it, I think. But let's see what the bidding turns up!' He finally let go of Lance and put his hand into his jacket pocket to pull out four envelopes.

*

'What's he doing?' asked Ben.

'Sealed bids,' said San. 'Best bid wins. This is Lance's chance now.'

They watched as Piggy took the envelopes and began to hand them out with blank sheets of paper.

Lance sidled back over to the egg and bent down to his briefcase. Vince wandered among the buyers, cajoling them and talking up the egg.

Sanjay switched on his lapel mic and hoped that Lance's earpiece was functioning. 'Cameras are good from all angles. Green light, *now!*' San switched off the mic.

As they hovered around the screen, it felt like watching a cup-final penalty. It could go either way.

'Come on, Lance! Get on with it!' hissed San.

Lance began to open the briefcase lid. Two more seconds and it would be over.

His face shot up and the briefcase lid slammed shut.

'What's going on?' Charlie demanded.

'How do I know? No sound! I knew I should have wired in some pick-ups. Damn!' San gritted his teeth. All they could do was watch.

*

Lance was convinced that his heart was about to audition for a heavy-metal rock band as it drummed away inside his chest. He was so close now. Just lift out the fake and do the switch. Then he was out of here.

A voice boomed in from his left. His head shot up and the lid of his case slammed shut.

'*Bal'shoe spa'siba za infar'matsiu?*'

The figure that spoke was one of the buyers; big bearded smile, huge tailored suit that indicated the man might be a billionaire but he still preferred the dumplings his grandma used to make, doused with a liberal dose of duck fat.

Lance was stuck. He was more than stuck. The words were Russian, he could work that out. But that was as far as his expertise went. How do you answer someone who says something you don't understand? He might as well rip the goatee off now and give up the game. Maybe he could just smile and nod his head. But the Russian looked as if he wanted to chat. Oh, wonderful. Lance saw his whole life flash in front of him, the parts he would never play, the reviews he would never get, the impressed girlfriends he would never snog...

'Excuse me!' shouted Vince, going red in the

face as he stalked over. 'I said in my messages to all buyers – English only!' He stared in the face of the bulky buyer. '*Comprende*, mate? I want to understand what's being said. No secret messages, no deals, nothing goes by except through me!'

The man stammered, 'Yes. Not problem,' and backed off. Lance was saved.

'Now, Mr Vinokurov, as our business is concluded, I do believe it's time for you and I to say goodbye.' Once again the arm gripped him around the shoulders, turned him one hundred and eighty degrees and propelled him towards the door.

San looked at Break. 'What was that all about?'

'Whatever it was, at least Lance is out of there.'

'Yeah, but without the egg we're back to square one,' said Charlie. Her father was no nearer freedom and Vince had got away with it.

At that moment, Piggy's phone rang.

'Yeah. I mean, yes? Who? Right! Vince, it's a Mr Vladimir Vinokurov. Says he's just got back from holiday and received our message...'

Vince frowned. His brain hadn't yet made the

connection. He grabbed the phone. 'Yes...yes. But you've just left the building...' Vince flipped the phone shut. 'Oh no. Oh no. Piggy! Dirk! The man's a fake!' They ran for the door that Lance had left seconds before.

12. PASS THE BALL

Friday 25 August, 8.15 pm

As Lance walked down the street ripping off the itchy fake beard and putting his glasses in a pocket, he heard a shout from behind him. He turned to see the doors of the warehouse slam open and two very angry bodyguards come barrelling towards him. He had a feeling they didn't want to stop and ask him the way to Madame Tussaud's. He ran as fast as he could, cradling the briefcase to his chest.

He dared to snatch another look behind. They were gaining and he heard Vince's shout echo all the way up the street.

'He's the only one who handled the egg! What the hell's going on? Get 'im, now!'

Lance was training to be an actor, not an

athlete. Why had he agreed to be involved in all this in the first place? He heard the men's hard breaths. A few more seconds and it would all be over.

'Lance! Chuck us the egg!' He looked up to see the gang pour out of an alley on their boards only a few metres ahead of him. Without thinking, he flipped the locks and jettisoned the case. He'd have to owe the props department on that one. In one swift movement he bowled the egg high in the air and it landed perfectly in Ben's outstretched hands.

'Yowza!' shouted Ben. 'Game on!'

Piggy's eyes did a double-take, horrified at the sight of what he thought was a multi-million-pound fragile artwork spinning through the air. 'Oh no! He's done a switch. That's the real egg!'

Lance sprinted off and the bodyguards paused. This lot didn't know what they were up against.

'This should be fun! Why don't you hand over the egg, like a good little boy?' said Piggy, flexing his muscles.

'Who wants to be the first with a broken leg?' asked Dirk, hoping rather optimistically that a volunteer might leap at the chance. He made a lunge at Ben, but the boy scooted out of the way as if the man was an annoying fly.

'Good try!' laughed Ben as he tossed the egg to Charlie. Piggy leapt up in the air, trying to catch it. If it dropped, his boss would go mental. Instead, he tripped over the kerb and bounced onto the pavement.

'Oh dear, it's Piggy in the middle and he's not doing very well. Awww!' Charlie threw the egg to Break, who took off on his board as the gang zoomed away down the street.

Seconds later Vince roared up in his Merc. 'Get in, you stupid fools! That's my merchandise they've got. We're not going to be beaten by some immature adolescents!' The doors slammed and the wheels screeched as Vince put his foot down.

'Looks like we've got motorised company!' shouted Break as they sped in formation down the street. 'We need traffic, plenty of it, and we need it now!' There were lights ahead of them and their luck was in as it seemed that half of London was in a rush to get somewhere that evening. Break ignored the red light and skidded sharp left, taking the main road that led downhill towards the river. 'Follow me!'

The rest of the gang veered off, trying to avoid the speeding cars and weaving motorbikes as they pushed with every last ounce of strength to take advantage of the steepening gradient. The only problem was that Vince was not playing by the rules. He followed them through the red light and happily blared his horn as he used the Merc more like a battering ram to push old biddies in ancient Fiestas out of the way and give several cyclists near heart attacks.

'He's gaining!' yelled Ben. San did his best to keep up, terrified of speed wobble but even more scared of what lay behind him if he slowed down.

'There!' shouted Break. The good old London bus. Break had explained the principle to them loads of times but he was the only one who'd ever been mad enough to try it out. Slipstreaming or street surfing was not the safest sport in the world, but it was based on obvious science. A massive brick of a bus barging through the streets left a nice air vacuum just behind it as it drove along. If you managed to get yourself into that space, the ride was almost frictionless. It was free energy, there for the taking.

The bus driver appeared to be on their side. With a nice long stretch ahead of her, she'd obviously decided that the sooner she got her shift over and done with, the quicker she could sink back a nice hot cup of tea. As a result, the bus was going at it like a racing car. And spread out behind, like a formation of geese, were the gang, backs bent over, riding the smooth tarmac as if they had inbuilt engines.

The Merc was stuck behind a white-van driver who knew that time was money and therefore dawdling was a well-paid occupation. Vince fumed, but there was nothing he could do. As they approached the bottom of the hill, Vince had had enough. The pavement was meant for walking on, but he decided to give it extra employment as an overtaking lane. In one quick move he veered round the van, narrowly missing one post-box and two pensioners. There, ahead of him, were the very easy targets of three boys and one girl.

Vince had no qualms about a bit of child squashing. Anyhow, they had the egg, and the egg was a priority. Serve them right for illegally skating in the middle of the street. His lawyers would have the case thrown out even before it got to court. He pressed down on the pedal and began to inch closer to the gang.

San looked round and panicked. 'Hey! We're about to be jam on toast!'

Break saw Vince creeping up on them. 'OK, after me – as the bus slows!' It was one of the last double-deckers with an open back and no doors.

Timing was crucial. As the bus slowed to turn at the bottom of the hill, Break lifted up the front of his board and leapt onto the platform of the bus. The passengers sitting at the back of the bus were too bored to be impressed, even though it was the stunt of a lifetime. He turned to lend a hand to the others as, one by one, they leapt through the air and onto the bus.

San was last. He couldn't pop an ollie if his life depended on it. His eyes were like a rabbit's, darting between Vince's bumper and the ever-growing gap between him and safety.

'Jump, damn it!' shouted Break.

There was a horrendous crunch and the Merc swerved, almost losing control.

'San!' Charlie screamed.

'That was close!' he whimpered, clinging on to her at the edge of the platform as the bus trundled off round the corner. His board had been turned into kindling, but he was safe.

'You need to work on your technique!' laughed Break as he led them upstairs. The conductor did his best to glare at them but they were happy to pay for tickets.

'Gives a new meaning to "catching the bus"!' said Ben.

They were all breathing heavily. Break lifted

the egg out from under his jumper. 'They can't get us while we're on the bus.'

'But what do we do now?' said San. 'Look behind us. They're going to follow us and then it'll be over! And I've lost my board. My dad'll kill me!'

'But don't you see – this could work to our advantage! They think we've got the real egg!' Even after everything that had gone wrong, Break's mind was on the move, computing the next scenario.

'How does that help us?' asked Charlie.

'In all sorts of ways,' Break smiled. 'Sit back and get your breath. The fun is only just starting!'

Ten minutes later, the right bus stop appeared. A quiet street. No one else getting on or off. Perfect. The Merc was a hundred metres behind. Vince obviously hadn't thought about why they'd make it so easy for him. His mind was on one thing only.

The gang disembarked, pretending not to see the Merc as it idled up behind them. The moment it got within ten metres, though, the chase resumed. Only this time, the gang split in four directions like the points of a compass. At least one of them should get away with it. As for the others, it was a risk they had to take.

Charlie knew exactly where she wanted to go. When she had started circus skills classes all those years ago, one of her friends lived in this area. After class they used to spend ages playing in the street, pretending they were performing to invisible audiences and using the alleys and ledges as their big top. She heard footsteps behind her. Not Piggy, he was too slow. She snatched a look. Dirk, with a confident smile on his face, that seemed to say she wouldn't get away this time.

The spot had to be here somewhere. As the dusk deepened, she scanned the street. Yes! There! Dirk was only metres behind her. It didn't seem to matter that she didn't have the egg. Anyway, it would have held her back.

It was a terrace of high brick houses with one strange feature. Right in the middle was a gap between two of them. A totally useless gap as it was too narrow to walk down, being barely more than 20 centimetres wide. Here goes! she thought as she leapt off her board and put her hands to the ground.

Dirk paused for a second, wondering why the stupid little girl was cartwheeling over the road. Oh well. Let her have her dumb show. But Dirk rubbed his eyes in disbelief as the girl vanished in the thin crack between the walls.

Charlie hadn't done this trick for years and if she was too big now, she'd smash her head up good and proper. But in the end, it was as smooth as riding a bike. She cartwheeled into the gap and carried on, up and over and over and up, spinning through space like a Catherine wheel. *Let's see Vince's man top this!* she thought as she exited the gap on the other side...straight into the waiting arms of Piggy.

13. TRAPPED

Friday 25 August, 9.15 pm

'Piggy in the middle, eh? I'll give you Piggy in the middle!' Piggy gripped Charlie's arm like a pincer. She tried kicking and scratching, but Piggy's smile only widened. 'My boss will be very, very pleased.'

'Will he? My dad told me you were stupid, Piggy. What good am I? You haven't got the egg!' said Charlie, out of breath. She wiped her free hand on her trousers, trying not to think about what had lain in the tiny alleyway through which she'd just cartwheeled.

'Never heard of swapsies, little girl? Let me explain it to you and then maybe, just maybe, the great Danny Cooper will get his daughter back in one piece. Here's how it goes. You ring your mates. They bring the egg. We swap. A mouthy girl for a money-making egg. Everyone goes home and it's happy ever after.'

Charlie looked up at Piggy's face in the dusk. Dirk and Vince were nowhere to be seen. If she could get them here quick enough, then maybe...

'Let my arm go, then. Can't do this phone one-handed!'

Piggy let go but stayed close in case she tried anything. She pulled out her phone and clicked it on. 'Oh, no. I thought I had plenty of credit. It's just cut me off!' Before Piggy could examine it, she shoved the phone back in her pocket.

The bodyguard shrugged his huge shoulders. 'Well, I suppose you can use mine then, but no fancy codes or nothin', unless you want me to break your stick of an arm.'

'Yeah. I promise.'

Piggy handed over his phone and she called Break, trying to keep the tears out of her voice. 'Hi. Look. Piggy's got me. What? No. Just bring the egg right now...Fleet Alley, you know where it is. Right. Got to go...' Her hand shook as she gave the phone back.

'I don't get it, Piggy! Why'd you turn on my dad like that? He'd done his time and then you framed him.' Charlie balled her fingers into fists.

'You'll have to ask Vince about that.' Piggy wasn't going to be drawn.

They waited two more minutes and then the gang turned up, skating out of the darkness, surrounding Piggy.

'Four of us and one of you!' said Break, pulling back his hoodie. 'I'd suggest you let go of our friend here. By the way, Charlie, here's your board.' He chucked it to her.

'Have you got the egg?' said Piggy. He seemed unconcerned by the threat.

'Aren't you the brave one!' said Break. 'Let's jump him on the count of three. One. Two...'

A figure stepped out of the shadows, holding something in his hand.

'I *am* impressed! Who would have thought four under-age little *kiddly-widdlies* could steal my egg? Excuse me for not applauding, but it's hard to clap with a gun in my hand.' The smile on Vince's face said victory was his.

Break put his hands down. 'And you'd use it? Against minors?'

'A *minor* problem, you could say, standing between me and that which I love? Yes, I would, though it would be a bit noisy round here. Dirk, get the car!'

Doors opened and Vince used the gun to indicate that the gang were to step inside. One by one they got in, clutching their skateboards.

'Oh, and could you please return what is rightfully mine?'

Ben stepped forward and reluctantly handed over the egg, which gleamed under the streetlight.

Vince stroked the egg as he sat in the front seat. The doors slammed and the gang were squeezed uncomfortably in the back with Dirk, who now held Vince's gun with a way-too-itchy finger. The journey back to the warehouse was silent. There was nothing to say. The car slowed down and stopped right outside the doors. If anything, the streets were even quieter. No pedestrians to shout out to, no helpful passing policemen.

Once inside, Piggy switched on the single light and went to fetch the other egg.

'Sit!' commanded Dirk and four bums hit the floor. Piggy set the egg up on the table and Vince put the fake next to it. He studied the two of them for a while and then looked at the gang.

'Very good. Very, very good. Your dad,' he motioned to Charlie, 'must still have connections.' He picked up the fake. 'But why did he think he'd get away with it? I mean, look at the real thing – see how shiny the rubies are! It looks almost new! Now that's what I call art. It's survived the test of time!' He put down the fake and picked up the real egg. Break tried not to look interested.

'And as for this heap of junk? He's tried to make it look old. Put a few scratches on it, somehow darkened the lustre of the stones. Doesn't fool me for a second. Your actor friend nearly had us all. But Vince doesn't lose, ever!' Vince lifted the Fabergé artefact up in the air as if he was about to smash it onto the concrete floor.

Four pairs of eyes stared and four pairs of lungs stopped breathing.

'On second thoughts...Piggy!' Piggy was eating the remains of a takeaway pizza. 'Chuck this!' Vince dropped the egg in the middle of the pizza as Piggy looked up, gutted that his meal had been both interrupted and squashed.

He grumbled a bit, but then closed the cardboard box over the egg and the uneaten pizza. 'Where, boss?'

'Ever heard of a bin, you thick-headed fool? And while you're about it, get rid of those pathetic toys. These *children* won't be needing them any more, I assure you!' Vince smiled and

Piggy scooped up the skateboards as if they were bits of rubbish. The gang were motioned outside again and into the car. Piggy locked the door, took a couple of steps down the alleyway where Ben and San had originally set up the cameras and lifted the lid of the bins. The boards went in first with a clatter. Then as he dropped the pizza-wrapped egg, there was the softest of thumps. The gang began to breathe again, even though the situation wasn't brilliant to say the least.

Once back in the car, Vince seemed undecided.

'Why don't we just do 'em, boss?' asked Dirk, eager to volunteer.

'Do 'em? *Do 'em*? You've been watching too many mafia films!' Vince slapped his head as if it was all too much. 'Your vocabulary is never going to win prizes, that's for sure,' he muttered. 'Look, there's a spot down by the river, you know the one I mean. Let's go.'

Dirk gave what passed for a smile but looked more like a gash cut across his face. 'Hope you're good at breathing underwater!' he hissed as the car drove off into the night.

The silence that descended filled the inside of the car like thick fog. What was there to say? After ten minutes, the car took a left and nosed its way between two tall brick buildings. The tarmac stopped and turned into a rough track as the car bumped into the shadows. They could smell the river straight ahead of them. Charlie shivered. They'd come this far and failed. It was over.

As the car ground to a halt Vince turned round. 'Right, mobile phones please! Wouldn't want you to think it's like the movies where you secretly summon help and the goodies ride to the rescue. Sorry, but real life ain't like that!' he snarled.

One by one, they handed over their phones. Charlie just stared at Vince and kept her hands in her pockets.

'Her phone's out of credit,' said Piggy.

'Yeah. The whole lot of them are about to be out of credit!' laughed Vince. He took the other phones and stamped on them a few times to make a point. Then the back door was opened and they stumbled out. Ben kept trying to engage Break with eye signals. Maybe they could try a move?

'Here's the thing...' said Vince, as if reading his mind. 'I'd love you to give it a go. You know, heroics, one last trick and all that. Dirk's an even better shot than me and he loves moving targets as, sadly, we don't get as much practice as we used to. So please, if you want to do anything exciting, now's your chance!'

Vince's words had the required effect. Ben felt all the energy leak out of him. They now stood at the edge of the embankment, looking out over the river. This stretch, away from the centre of London and the posh converted warehouses, was dark and oily. The tide was low and Break could make out what passed for a beach down below.

'More shopping trolleys! I told you they'd multiply,' said Ben. No one laughed. The gun in Dirk's hand indicated a ladder built into the river wall. Break led the gang down the slippery rungs until all of them stood on the slightly squashy pebbled sand. They could hear the low roar of the river only a few metres away.

'A lovely spot to get away from it all, don't you think?' Vince waved his arms around as if he was on a beach in Spain and not some god-forsaken spit of land in the old industrial heartland of the city. 'My colleagues will now help you get truly knotted!' Vince chuckled to himself as the gang found themselves being expertly trussed up and then tied tightly to an old docking ring. Break grimaced, remembering how a similar ring had helped him escape only two weeks before.

'Yes. Only this time, you won't get away. No convenient sewer mouths, I think you'll find,' said Vince, reading his thoughts. He stood back to admire his bodyguards' handiwork.

Charlie strained against the ropes and tried to wriggle around.

'Not much point doing that!' said Vince. 'Professional-grade climbing rope – it'll stop a sixteen-stone man in freefall – so you don't present much of a challenge!'

'How could you do this?' demanded Charlie.

'Look, it's only business. Your father was the perfect scapegoat. He's hardly Mr Innocent. And when I heard he was free, I knew it was an opportunity I had to take. Let's face it, little lady, prison is the best place for losers like him. And as for the egg, I'm the one who stole it, so I have to be the one who profits. I'm very sorry you got in my way, but look, I'm no murderer!'

'How can you say that?' said Break.

'Easily. I just did. I'm off out of here. It's not me doing the dirty work, but our old friend the river!' As Vince spoke, the water began to well around the bottoms of their shoes. Vince motioned to his bodyguards and they climbed the ladder away from danger.

'If you fancy screaming, don't let me stop you. But there's not a lot of people round here at this time of night, and anyhow, the water will soon calm you down. Night night, sleep tight! It's been good doing business with you!' Vince vanished with his cronies over the top of the embankment, leaving four children and a rapidly rising river.

14. HIDDEN VOICES

Friday 25 August, 10.15 pm

Vince found himself polishing the enamel of the egg with his shirt sleeve. The weight of it in his hands felt reassuring. He stared at the egg. It glittered back at him. It was as close to love as Vince would ever get. 'I feel a bit sorry for them, boys.'

'You don't mean that, Boss?' said Piggy.

'No, you're right. I don't. Piggy, get on the phone and rearrange the meeting, and this time with the real egg!'

As the car drove off into the darkness, Piggy got down to business.

A few minutes later Vince's dreams of riches were rudely interrupted. 'Whoever put the *Teletubbies* theme tune on their phone better shut it off right now unless they want to be eating their mobile!' he fumed.

'Not me!' said Dirk.

'Nor me!' protested Piggy.

'You sure you broke all those kids' phones?'

'Yes, boss. That's what I do. Break things and make sure they stay broken!' said Dirk. He pulled the car to a halt and turned on the overhead light. 'Boss...it seems to be coming from you. I thought you didn't have a phone?'

'I don't, stupid!' His hands searched the pockets of his suit and around the inside of the car where he was sitting.

'I think it's coming from there!' Piggy pointed a quivering finger at the egg.

'Yeah, Carl Fabergé was into Tinky Winky and Laa-Laa land. His favourite programme, I heard.' Vince was worried though. He held the egg up to his ear. Sure enough, the tinny little song seemed to be coming straight out of the jewelled treasure. 'Impossible!'

Matters got worse. The song suddenly stopped and a tinny Teletubby voice from inside spoke up. 'Eh-oh, Vince!' it said three times and then stopped.

Vince almost dropped the egg as his eyes went wide. There was a sudden scraping noise from the bottom of the jewel. Vince turned over the egg to see a flashing sign appear among the fake pearls and glass rubies.

Piggy did all of them the favour of reading it out loud. '"Made in England", it says! What does that mean, boss?'

Vince took Piggy's ear and twisted it around until he squealed. 'I know that I never hired you for your intelligence, Piggy. But for once, just for once, keep your greasy little trap shut.' Vince gave one last vicious pull and let go of the ear. Luckily for Piggy it was still attached to his head.

'What it means, Fat-For-Brains, is that we have been done, good and proper. Dirk, turn this car round and get to the river, quick. We need to ask a few questions and get a few answers before the river fills their mouths with water!'

Dirk did as he was told. He had always dreamed of being a racing driver and now he treated the backstreets of London like his own personal race-track. He skidded round corners, ignored crossroads and generally accelerated all the way as Piggy tried to keep the contents of his pizza where they belonged – in his stomach. The car lurched down the alley and screeched to a stop. Vince leapt out and ran for the embankment. They'd only been gone for half an hour, surely not time enough for the tide to rise? He leant over the parapet and scanned the darkness below. The beach had gone, almost as if it had never been there. At that moment the moon made a helpful appearance.

No! It couldn't be! There was the docking ring, glinting dully in the half-light, just above the water level. But instead of children, all he could see were coils of rope, slithering out into the water like a family of dead eels. 'Impossible!' he roared. Break, Charlie, Ben and San had gone.

'Search the area! Now!' he screamed at Dirk and Piggy. They did as they were told, scurrying around in what soon proved to be a totally fruitless exercise.

Vince paced up and down, unable to believe he'd been beaten again. 'Think, Vince, think!... Oh! For once, I am stupid, stupid, stupid. The egg was a fake, boys – and that means...'

Dirk got there before him. 'The other one...the one Piggy threw away!'

'Yes, precisely. The warehouse, now!'

'I'm on it, Boss!' said Dirk, jumping into the front seat. Piggy almost fell out of the back as the car ripped out of the alleyway and went screeching off towards the site of their greatest mistake.

The gang felt the water rise above their ankles. 'This doesn't look good,' said San.

'Do you always make obvious statements, gadget boy?' asked Break. 'Got any bits of high-tech stuff to free us from death by drowning?'

'Nah. *Gizmoid* magazine is a bit short of that particular type of equipment.'

Ben flexed his muscles, but the rope just bit deeper. 'While you two are having a nice chat, how about we try to actually do something?'

'What?' snapped Break. 'Think about it. The trussed-up turkey doesn't leap out of the oven, you know. And that's the stage we're at...'

'Are you finished yet, boys? If you are, could you be quiet so I can concentrate?' Charlie grunted.

'Oooooh! The girlie's getting angry!' said Ben. 'Got a master plan up your sleeve by any chance?'

'No, but what I do have up my sleeve is a very flexible double-jointed arm, attached to a body that's been training in circus skills for ever...'

'Don't tell me, you aim to do your underwater trapeze act?' Ben was ribbing Charlie, but as the water rose to their waists, fear began to flood his veins.

'No, Ben. But one of the acts I started to take lessons in was escapology. I read all the old Houdini books, you know.'

'Yeah, but he cheated. Secret compartments, split ropes, hidden buttons.'

'Not always. The trick with rope is to treat it as a puzzle. If you know the moves you can find your way out.' She grunted again, then breathed out sharply. 'It's amazing the difference a bit of breath can make. It's the oldest trick in the book. Breathe in and hold as much air in your lungs as they tie you up. It makes you bigger, no matter how tight they make the knots. Then you breathe out and work on your snake impression!' Charlie carried on wriggling as the boys stared in amazement. One of her arms slipped from the rope as if it was a tiger walking out of a zoo.

'Way to go!' said Break, impressed.

'But there's always a price to pay...' Break could see that the rope had cut the skin on her forearm as blood seeped out and dripped into the water.

Fingers set to work and soon Charlie's other arm was free.

'Come on, girl. Get on with it!' San panicked as the water rose up his chest.

'Give me a chance. These knots are evil and my fingers are freezing!' The river ignored all of them, doing its job. Break could feel the occasional bump as objects floated into him. He tried not to imagine what they were. Most of them had free arms by now and helped work the rope. But still their legs were trapped. As the shortest member of the gang, San now had water up to his chin. In a few seconds, he wouldn't be able to breathe any more. He opened his mouth to scream but Charlie slapped him, hard. 'Stay calm!' she ordered. 'I will get you out, I promise! If the water goes over your head, hold your breath.'

There was nothing for it. She had no choice. Charlie leant forward and dived under the murky water. If it was difficult to see above, it was pure murk down here. She closed her eyes and prayed her fingers remembered the moves. She pretended she was in the glass water tank at the circus doing the Dice with Death chain trick, with the audience also holding their breath in sympathy with the mad young girl. Except at the circus a diver with an air bottle was always on hand, just out of sight, in case anything went wrong. But now there was no back-up, and she could feel the strain in her lungs, the mad desire to let go and breathe in the foul water. Just one more, one more knot, and she could swim up and take a bow to welcome applause!

There! The last bit of rope came free! She pushed San with all her remaining strength until he kicked and floated to the surface.

'Urghhhh!' he spluttered, spitting out water with unidentifiable bits. 'Thanks Charlie! You...saved my life.'

Charlie was too tired to respond. The others trod water and watched the rope, still attached to the docking ring, billow out down the current, just another bit of river flotsam. One by one they swam to the ladder and began the climb back to the safety of solid ground. They were cold, soaked, half-dead, miserable, but free!

15. EGGED ON

Friday 25 August, 10.15 pm

'You ever read *The Swamp Thing*?' asked Ben as they ran along the dark streets, dripping on the ground.

'No,' said Break, sneezing. 'But I get your point. Just remind me to stay away from sewers *and* rivers in future. I think I'm developing an allergy! And what am I going to tell my mum this time?'

'Hang on a second, you lot!' San hurried to keep up. 'Aren't we forgetting something?'

'Yes. You, slowcoach!' Charlie tugged San's sleeve but he stopped dead and bent over, panting hard.

'No. The warehouse can wait for a couple of minutes. It's time to see if the remote control still works.'

'What are you talking about?' said Ben.

'The egg, remember? Theodore's work of art, with its extra features thanks to yours truly.' San pulled the fat chronograph watch off his wrist and turned it over. 'Waterproof to thirty metres. I do hope so.' Next to the engraved back was a small red button. 'Shall I set it off?'

The others gathered around, and for the first time in a while there were smiles on their faces. San pressed the button. Nothing happened. 'Let's hope it works.'

'I'd love to see the look on Vince's face when the egg starts singing to him!' said Charlie. 'Why couldn't you get a built-in camera?'

San stared at Charlie. 'It's not James Bond, you know!' He put the watch back on. 'Right – let's get to that warehouse before he works it all out!'

Dirk was pleased with himself. As he pulled the handbrake and a very green-looking Piggy tumbled out of the back, he pressed the stop button on his watch. Eight minutes and thirty-five seconds. As he began to bask in the warmth of imaginary applause, Vince punched him on the shoulder.

'Check the building. Don't want any nasty surprises from those kids, do we?' Vince was very careful to make sure Dirk was the first to enter the dark entrance porch as he hid behind his bodyguard's bulk. No one could accuse Vince of being a coward and live to tell the tale. But thugs were hired as human shields and he might as well take advantage.

The building was empty, the single light bulb only showing cases of the wrong sort of egg – the chocolate ones that melted in your mouth and cost a lot less than the jewel he'd stolen.

Piggy walked into the room, his hands covered in bits of pepperoni and stringy cheese.

'Would you stop licking your fingers, please, Piggy? You give a bad name to the human race!'

'Sorry, Boss. Felt a bit peckish and thought I'd finish off my dinner.'

'If I wanted a conversation about your disgusting eating habits, I would have asked! Was it there?'

'I searched everywhere. Honest. I even got inside the bin. The egg's gone.' Piggy cringed, knowing that this wasn't the answer Vince wanted to hear.

Vince couldn't contain himself. He lifted up one of the pallets of chocolate eggs and threw it at Piggy. The eggs spattered onto the ground and the foil tore to reveal a sickly, sugary gloop. As if by instinct, Piggy picked up one of the fallen eggs and began to eat it.

'You're useless. The whole thing is a waste.' A vein bulged ominously on Vince's forehead. Dirk wondered if it would burst. 'Beaten by prepubescent prats! What do you propose we do, Piggy?'

'Dunno, Boss!'

'No, you don't. You never did. Maybe I should go to the police. What do you think of that?'

Dirk was worried. His master was always a few biscuits short of a packet, but now he was sounding deranged. Vince and the word 'police' never normally occurred in the same sentence.

Vince had the fake egg in his hand. The singing had stopped ages ago, but the sign at the bottom still flashed away merrily. Somehow, even though it was a piece of junk, he couldn't chuck it. 'Come on. Shut this place up and let's go.' He strode out of the warehouse and headed for the car.

A siren began to wail nearby, but Vince's mind was elsewhere. As he stood in front of the building, a police car drew up, and its headlights framed the glittering egg perfectly.

'Evening, sir,' said the policeman as he cautiously opened the car door and stood up. 'We had some reports of a speeding vehicle that seems to match the description of this one. Is this your vehicle, sir?'

There was a short silence. Vince blinked. Then his mind got into gear. 'Yes. Yes. Terribly sorry. I heard there had been a break-in at my business premises. I asked my driver to step on it in case we could catch the criminals still at it. I did ask him to not go over the speed limit but, like you, officer, I was keen to see justice done.' Vince gave his most sincere smile. The copper seemed to be falling for it.

'I see, sir. And have you caught the perpetrators?'

'No. It looks like they got away.' Vince gave a shake of his head.

'And did they steal anything of value?'

'Y...no. No. I was lucky this time.'

'Well. I think your driver was very lucky no cameras caught him. And what if a pedestrian had been crossing the road? We can't encourage taking the law into your own hands, eh?'

'Absolutely. I am very sorry, officer. The business has been very stressful recently and the last thing I needed was a theft.' Vince played the part brilliantly. He was a man in a suit, worthy of respect, doing his best to uphold law and order. Now, if only the smarmy uniform would get back in the car, he could carry on with the business of dealing out revenge.

The officer paused and looked at Vince again. 'That's a very interesting object you're holding in your hand.'

Vince looked down. The egg sat there in plain view, the stones glinting in the halogen headlights. His fast-thinking brain had no answer.

'Funny that. My missus loves those crime programmes – you know, the ones you get members of the public phoning in on. Normally, after a shift on the streets, I wouldn't be bothered. I get to see enough lowlifes in the day job. But the other night, well, they were going on about this egg made by a bloke called Flabbyjee.'

Vince couldn't help himself. 'It's pronounced Faberjay!'

'You got it. So there I was, with a nice cup of tea and a Hobnob, all cuddled up to the wife and I thought to myself – wouldn't it be amazing to find the mastermind who nicked that? It's gotta be worth ten million at least and the reward would add very nicely to my pension. We all have our daydreams, don't we, sir?'

Vince did not nod.

The policeman obviously enjoyed the sound of his own voice. 'So, here I am, back on shift, following up calls about a speeding car and where does it lead me, I ask you?'

'I don't know, officer. Where does it lead you?' said Vince, feeling more and more hopeless. He'd sensed that Piggy and Dirk had vanished long ago into the shadows. So much for loyalty.

'Well. It leads me here, to you, sir...and to that object in your hand, which looks remarkably like the egg that was stolen from Somerset House four weeks ago.'

16. THE TWIST

The cop's smile was wider and more self-satisfied than any Cheshire Cat. Vince sensed a greed similar to his own and wondered if at that very second the officer was working out what to spend his reward on.

But Vince hadn't climbed to the top of the greasy pole to slide so easily down. In fact, if anything, the kids had done him a favour.

'Yes!' he said in response to the cop's last comment. 'This egg is beautiful, almost a work of art!' Vince's voice sounded confident – too confident.

Normally, when a policeman was about to nick someone, the villain would at least have the decency to look slightly downcast. The smirk on

Vince's face did not fit. The officer ploughed on, regardless. 'That it is, sir. And I'm afraid I'm going to have to ask you...'

Vince interrupted the officer, and his next words well and truly wiped the smile off his face. 'As I was saying, *almost* a work of art.' Vince turned the egg upside down. The 'Made in England' sign still flashed away merrily. 'It was a wonderful exhibition – though a terrible shame about the stolen egg. Still, if I couldn't get the real thing, I was so excited to purchase this fantastic replica for my mother. She's very poorly, you know.'

The officer's face fell. 'No, I didn't know, sir,' he replied through gritted teeth.

'Anyhow, I'm sure this will make her day. Something glittery, a reminder of different times. Might even add a bit of glamour to her bedside!' Vince began to enjoy himself. 'Was there anything else I could help you with, *officer*?'

The policeman was well and truly beaten. The summer cruise he'd paid for in his mind for him and his wife vanished into thin air. For a second, he thought about booking the man for speeding, but it was late and it would mean more forms to fill in back at the station.

'I'll let you off this time, but mind how you

drive your vehicle from now on.'

Vince nodded, pretending that he'd learnt his lesson, and the police car drove off into the darkness. He breathed a sigh of relief. It was time to hunt down his spineless employees for one last job. He'd been tricked one too many times. The kids would get what was coming.

'My house deserves better than you lot dripping all over the carpet!' sighed Charlie. 'And could you please leave your boards outside – they're filthy!'

The other three were too tired to complain that Charlie was playing the role of mother. Break and Ben trooped outside, dropped their boards and came back in. Everyone was exhausted.

'You lot, see if you can find some dry clothes in my dad's cupboard. I'm going to check on my mum.' After going upstairs Charlie towelled her wet hair, cleaned and bandaged the cut on her arm, and fussed around the kitchen getting the kettle on the go. Nearly dying was bad enough, but catching a cold was not on the agenda.

The egg sat glaring at her on the worktop. 'Silly thing!' she whispered. 'All the trouble you've caused us!' She took a dishcloth and wiped a bit of stray cheese from the miniature crown at the top. The boys came back into the kitchen looking like a trio of clowns with oversized shirts and floppy trousers. Charlie couldn't help smiling. 'Well, I knew my dad had put on a bit of weight in prison! Hang on a second!' She pulled out her phone, shook a few drops from it and clicked it into camera mode.

'Smile and say mozzarella!' The phone took its silent picture.

'I thought your phone was bust!' said Ben.

'Never believe everything I say, boy! I wrapped it in a plastic bag.'

'You are unbelievable!' hissed Ben between his teeth. Charlie gave a little bow and made everyone's tea.

'Right!' said Break as they sat in the living room. 'San, you ring Lance and pass the message on to Danny. The rest of us need to sort out what to do with this dangerous jewel!'

'Won't Vince come after us, now he knows we've got it?' said Ben.

'Good point. We have to get the egg out of here. I know it's been a long night, but it's not over yet. We should take it to Theodore's place – that's about as safe as we can get. We need to move fast.'

'I can't wait to see the look in his eyes – the

jewel his great-grandfather crafted! Wow!'
Charlie was excited. The tea, with plenty of
sugar, also worked wonders. She passed round a
tray of toast and Marmite. After their battle with
the river they were starving.

San tried to speak with a full mouth. 'Why
don't we just take the egg to the police? Let them
sort out Vince and then we can get back to our
boring, everyday lives.'

'Not yet,' said Break. 'Theodore said
something...I want to check it out. Charlie,
could you lend your old board to San?'

The toast was polished off, even the crusts, and
Charlie handed out some Twixes to keep them
going. Two minutes later they headed out again
with the egg carefully wrapped in an old
sheepskin and carried in Break's shoulder bag.
If they went for it, they could be at Theodore's
in twenty minutes, max. At least no one was
chasing them and they flew like birds in
formation along the black tarmac.

They were dead tired and maybe that's why their
eyes were not quite sharp enough to spot the car,
headlights turned off, that pulled out of the
alleyway and crawled behind them. German
engineering meant that the vehicle was almost
silent, which suited the driver's purpose perfectly.

17. SURPRISES ALL ROUND

Friday 25 August, 11.30 pm

The alley was deserted and the only sound was the turning of street wheels on paving stones. If Break had his way, he'd ban walking altogether as an inconvenient and outdated form of transport. He tucked the board under his arm and dived into the doorway. The others followed.

The man who greeted them at the door could not hide the smile that threatened to break out all over his face.

'Come! It is late, but sleep is for ze lazy and young!' Theodore greedily eyed the bulge in Break's shoulder bag, but his manners would not let him jump to conclusions. He herded them like sheep up the stairs and closed the door behind him with obvious relief. 'You have many things to tell me, but first, good, strong coffee, I think!' He indicated for the gang to make themselves at home, then busied himself putting the kettle on the ring and dolloping spoons of grounds into a tin coffee pot that had seen better days. The smell as he added the water revived them all.

Small glass cups were assembled on a tray and the coffee poured. Finally, he heaped two spoons of sugar into each cup. 'Pah! Milk is such an English veakness viz coffee. Zis is how you should drink!' The only light came from a couple of table lamps bent over the workbench in the corner and the rest of the vast room fell into shadow. If it wasn't for the caffeine, Charlie would have comfortably sunk into the sofa and nodded off. It seemed this day would never end.

Break took a few sips of his drink and undid his shoulder bag. As he unwrapped the sheepskin, a sigh escaped from Theodore. For a few seconds, he couldn't speak. Break held the egg out and Theodore gingerly accepted the glittering parcel.

'Ah! My hand is sure, but zat of my great-grandfazer makes all else a pale imitation!' He lifted his spectacles and peered closer. 'Even ze leaves on zese legs are veined viz rose diamonds. I play viz paste and glass but zis is...vunderful. I never thought to hold such a thing in my own hands.' As he lovingly cradled the family treasure, Break filled him in on the evening's events.

'And he vould have left you to ze mercy of ze rising tide?'

Four serious faces nodded in response.

'Zis man is animal and you are only children! If I was general of army, I vould give you many medals! Yes! But now, you bring zis egg to me, vhy?'

Charlie spoke up. 'My father said you told him a story, passed down through your family. This egg...'

But Theodore suddenly looked worried as he brushed Charlie's words aside. 'Stories, stories. Zis egg is real, and it does not belong to us. Zat is ze only story I am interested in. I have been to jail vunce, and vunce is enough.' It was as if he was holding a poisoned chalice. 'Shouldn't ve take zis to ze police now? Vot if...'

The door slammed open and Theodore almost dropped the egg on the hard ground.

'Yeah. What if I'd happened to follow you from your house, Miss Cooper? And what if you'd all been too tired to bother looking behind you?

And what if I'd picked your downstairs lock? Tut tut! Only a three-lever – a toddler could have done it. And what if I'd finally found what's rightfully mine. And what if I now ask you to please, pretty please, return it to me?' The voice finished with a snarl and the speaker stepped out of the shadows. There was a gun and the gun was attached to an arm and the arm belonged to a very angry Vince. As if things couldn't get any worse, Dirk and Piggy brought up the rear.

'You must be ze oaf who has so little art in his soul zat his only solution is to steal it!'

'Brave words from an old man,' said Vince. He peered into the gloom and spotted the workbench. 'Anyhow, coming up with a fake hardly makes you the artist, eh?'

Break felt like punching himself. It wasn't as if they were trained spies, able to sniff anyone following them. They'd got away from Vince twice, but third time unlucky. There was only one exit and three well-grown thugs against a few kids and a doddering goldsmith. The situation did not look good.

'The thing is,' said Vince, breaking the silence, 'I'll finally get my assets returned to me, but that leaves yet more loose ends. You lot obviously didn't have a problem with untying a few knots.

But I've not yet seen the human being who can evade a high-velocity bullet!' He screwed a silencer onto the end of the barrel as if it was all in a day's work. Break noticed he was wearing gloves.

'You mean to shoot us, including zese innocent children?' Theodore spluttered.

'Less of the *innocent*, old man. As they say in the movies, it's just business. No hard feelings, eh?' He raised the gun. 'The way I see it, or the way the police will see it, is like this: bitter old man, recently freed from jail, lures kids to his flat, shoots the lot and then tops himself. Oh what a tragedy. Who volunteers to go first?'

'I think you do!' said a voice, leaping out of the shadows.

Two things happened at once. Vince pulled the trigger and a bullet shot out of the muzzle. At the same time, his face went a funny colour and he collapsed on the floor. Behind him stood Danny Cooper with a rather heavy Russian tea urn in his hand. The bullet shattered a mirror on the wall and showered the gang with tiny glass shards.

Dirk and Piggy stood and watched their boss slowly slide onto the ground. Piggy began to move towards Danny and events seemed to unfold in slow-mo. As the gang watched transfixed, Break flew from the sofa towards Piggy with a determined look on his face. In the next second, tears sprang from Piggy's eyes and his hands shot downwards to protect himself. But Piggy was too late. Break's foot had connected with a very vulnerable part of Piggy's anatomy. Piggy gave a high-pitched screech and fell writhing onto his boss.

Two of the men were now down, leaving only Dirk standing. He tried to look menacing. Then his lips moved silently as if counting how many figures now strode purposefully towards him. He was outnumbered and the door behind was blocked by his old colleague, Danny Cooper, who held the Russian bit of lumpy brass in his hand like a weapon.

'It's the boss's fault!' he whined as they closed in. After a few thumps and even more moans, the resulting pile-up on the floor almost looked artistic. With shaking hands, Theodore punched in the number for the police on his phone while Danny picked up the gun and trained it on the three men who had been smiling only seconds before.

'Way to go, Break! That was one sick move!' said Ben with admiration in his voice.

Break looked rather pleased. 'Well, it beats a fakie heelflip any day!'

'Have you ever thought of taking up martial arts? With a kick like that, you'd be sponsored in no time! Break...the boy who can skate *and* kick ass!'

Danny shuffled over to his daughter, keeping the men in his sights. 'I should never have got you into all this.' He picked some of the glass out of her hair, then pulled a tiny sliver out of her cheek and wiped the blood with his sleeve.

'You didn't get me into all this, Dad. If you want to blame anyone, blame Vince!' She hugged him and they stood there while flashing blue lights lit up the room from outside and sirens broke the silence.

The door slammed open again and suddenly the room was filled with police in bullet-proof vests and visors.

'Drop the gun, sir. Now!'

Danny slowly put the gun on the ground. 'It's not me you want. Here are the real criminals!' He pointed at the figures huddled pathetically on the ground. But all the police had seen as they entered was a man holding a gun and unconscious bodies. Before Danny could say anything more, the gun was kicked away from him and he was lying face-down with his arm twisted painfully behind his back.

'What do you think you're doing?' screamed Charlie. 'My dad's just saved our lives!'

Vince was coming to. He felt the bump on his head and took in the scene immediately. 'Help! I've been attacked... That Cooper's a...a madman. He nicked the egg and now he's going to kill us all!' The lies spilled out into the room and filled the sudden silence. They sounded good.

'Zis is all not true!' spat Theodore.

'And that man...' Vince pointed at Theodore, 'is a forger. They cooked up a plan together. The kids are in on it too! I've been assaulted and my colleagues attacked for simply trying to investigate a break-in at my factory.' He was on shaky ground here, but no one seemed to notice.

One of the police helped Vince to his feet. The thief played the righteous businessman to perfection.

'If you don't believe me – there's the proof!' and Vince pointed at the old Russian.

Theodore still held the real Fabergé egg in his hand, an egg that had been stolen four weeks before in the hands of a convicted criminal.

'Good work, boys!' The senior officer indicated

for his team to stand down. 'We've caught the gang.' He strode up to Danny. 'Who would have thought it, Cooper! It's bad enough that you never learnt your lesson, but to involve your daughter and a bunch of now not-so-innocent secondary school kids! That's low, that is. Well, the only eggs you'll be having will be boiled and the only bars you'll be getting acquainted with will be made of metal!'

18. IT ALL GOES MOBILE

Saturday 26 August, 12.15 am

'Wait a second!' cried Charlie and reached down towards her pocket. Instinct and training meant that before her hand could even begin to delve, six firearms were pointed at her body.

'Stop right there, young lady!'

Charlie looked up and saw the guns. She froze.

The senior officer motioned Charlie to put her hands up. Instead, she turned and faced him directly.

'No. I'm not a criminal and nor is my dad. Fine if you want to point a whole arsenal of guns at me, but I'm not about to pull a fast one on you, OK?'

Everyone gawped at her. What was she on about?

'Do what the man says!' hissed Ben. 'This is no

time for your stupid tricks, girl! You might be a pain in the butt, but I'd rather have you annoying me while you're still alive...'

Her father tried to squirm out of the grip of his handcuffs. 'Leave it, Charlie. Please!'

Charlie ignored her dad and stared out the senior officer. 'Can I get my phone now, please?' She didn't wait for an answer. As if daring the squad to shoot, she slowly and carefully put her hand into her pocket. No one breathed. It was like a game of tennis as the heads swivelled from Charlie to the senior officer and back again. What order should he give? One word and it would all be over.

The man pulled up his visor. His face was red with anger. He was at least twice the size of this gobby little schoolgirl and tactically speaking, unless she had *Matrix*-style superpowers, his force had the upper hand. But the girl was stubborn and she didn't look like a mad markswoman. He thought for a second about his own daughter and the grief she'd given him since she'd turned teenage. Their last fight had been about getting a belly-button piercing. He was hardly going to shoot his own daughter over that.

'Hold your fire!' he announced.

Charlie nodded briefly at the man and pulled out a very un-dangerous flip-top mobile. She proceeded to open it up.

The officer had had enough. 'You can make your call when you're at the station. There's no one going to ride to your rescue now.'

But the words bounced into thin air. 'These new-gen mobiles do so much more than make calls. You can download songs, pick up emails, surf the web, take pictures and, even better, the video quality has really improved...'

What was she wittering on about? Break wondered if, with all the pressure of her dad and the problems with her mum, she'd finally gone off the rails. Somehow, though, her voice kept everyone mesmerised.

She punched a few buttons. 'As I said, the video is really quite something. Take this bit of filming I did earlier this evening...' On cue, she pressed 'play' and a tinny voice filled the room:

'Your father was the perfect scapegoat. He's hardly Mr Innocent. And when I heard he was free, I knew it was an opportunity I had to take. Let's face it, little lady, prison is the best place for losers like him. And as for the egg, I'm the one who stole it, so I have to be the one who profits.'

Charlie pressed 'pause'. 'I do hope you recognise the voice and the figure behind it?' She passed the phone to the senior officer, who didn't know if he wanted to congratulate the girl for her cleverness or stamp on the phone for being shown up.

'There's plenty more, as when I took that little film, your innocent businessman here was in the process of tying us up so that Mother Thames could drown us.'

Vince jumped in. 'This is lies. All lies! Cooked up by one of those computer whizzkids. They can do anything these days.' His voice rose in pitch as six members of Her Majesty's finest swivelled their guns to finally train them on the truly guilty.

'You'd better release Mr Cooper...' said the officer, wearily. 'It seems that...we had the wrong man.'

Danny rubbed his wrists as the cuffs were taken off. 'Sorry would be nice!' He ran over to take his daughter in his arms. Nobody spoke. 'Yeah. You lot don't do apologies very well.'

The officer tried to reassert control. 'I'll still need you all to come down to the station for your witness statements. And shall we get that egg into safekeeping?' He reached out towards Theodore.

'I'm sorry,' said Charlie, though she wasn't at all. 'There's one last favour I want to ask you.'

By now Vince and Dirk were being marched out of the room. Piggy was still in obvious pain as he shuffled along behind them. He took one look back only to see Break give him a wink. If his head could have hung any lower, it would have.

'It's the egg,' said Charlie. 'We solved the crime, recovered precious lost property, and all I ask is that you give Theodore a few minutes with it. By the way, I don't think I've introduced you. This is Theodore Perchin, great-grandson of Michael Perchin, the man who made Lilies of the Valley.'

Theodore gave a little bow.

'Don't worry, he won't replace it with a fake. But there's more to that egg than meets the eye.'

Despite himself, the senior officer was hooked. Half his team had departed, but the others drew closer as they shouldered their pistols.

'Ah!' said Theodore. 'You still believe in stories, do you, young girl?'

Charlie thought for a second. 'Well. You told it to my dad and my dad shared it with us. That same tale has passed down the generations to you. Don't you want to know if it's true or not?'

'Ze true jeweller is a maker of puzzles. He puts togezer objects of such intricacy, all vill forever ask "how is it made?" Zis is ze magic of our craft. Please, let me take ze egg to my vorkbench.' The police team parted as he carried the egg to the far wall and trained his work lamp onto the glittering surface.

'It is all so long ago. Anozer time, ven it vos hard to rise above your station. How could a humble goldsmith fall in love viz an empress? It vos impossible, ze stuff of fairy tales!' Theodore twisted the pearl on top of the miniature crown and the egg unfurled its treasure. The miniature portraits of the Tsar and his daughters Olga and Tatiana rose up.

'And yet, every Perchin from time immemorial knows of his secret love. And if it must be secret, vot better place to hide it zan a gift?'

He lifted the whole egg up and gently shook it. There was no sound, though the pearls that hung like tiny fragile flowers looked as if they would break off and float gently to the ground.

'If his heart vos broken, zen zat is ze message he must have given to her. Ve too must break zis heart, to get, as it vere, to ze heart of ze matter.' Theodore hummed and hawed, and then a smile spread slowly across his face. 'Oh! Very, very good! Let us give it a try.' He pressed his thumb onto one of the pearls and Charlie thought she could see something shift. Then, before anyone could stop him, Theodore gripped the egg hard in both hands and pulled it apart as if he was opening a book.

The senior officer looked on in horror. This old man was in the act of destroying one of the rarities of history! But instead of falling to pieces, the egg merely gave the tiniest of clicks as it happily split into two halves. Nothing broke, no pearly bits or gold fell off. And what lay in the centre of the egg, possibly untouched for nearly a hundred years, astounded them all.

Charlie was the first to speak. 'It's...beautiful!' Even the hardened police response team couldn't disagree.

She reached forward. 'May I?'

'It is possible you vill be ze first person to do so since ze Empress herself!'

'You think she would have worked it out?'

'I vould hope so, in my heart, zat at last she knew ze yearning of zis humble man. As to vether she approved or even more, if zey met, vell...no book vill ever tell us...' Theodore watched as Charlie plucked the pink-orange translucent stone from its heart-shaped, velvet-lined compartment, nestled deep inside the egg. The stone was almost as big as her thumb. For a second, she fell back in time, imagining the grand lady finding out about her secret admirer.

'Of course. It is an oval cut! Vun egg inside anozer. But zis holds ze final secret – a pink sapphire known as *padparadscha* – ze rarest of stones. It is like holding a shard of sunset!'

The tiny facets gleamed under the lamplight, dazzling all present.

Theodore looked around at the assembled faces. 'Zere. Ve have found it. Come, young Miss Cooper, let us return ze egg to its nest for now and let ze police take very good care of it!' He turned to stare at the senior officer.

'And I insist zat zese children are taken back to zeir families and any questions can vait until morning, yes?' Theodore gently took the stone from Charlie and placed it back in the egg. He pushed the two halves together and then handed it over. The day was done. It was time to go home.

19. FEAST YOUR EYES ON THIS!

**Saturday 2 September, 3.00 pm –
one week later**

It was a sound he was almost homesick for. The click of wheels on concrete and wood, the cheers, the music pumping out rhythm over the speakers. Most people had their tribe and Break was happy to admit to anyone who asked that he was content among his own species. The only problem with this place being so good was that it attracted the cream of skaters from all over the city, which meant that here he was just one of the crowd and not top dog.

He looked around at the crumbling concrete ramps, the bent plywood verts, the rusty rails, the graffitied walls and ripped sofas in the chill-out zone. Overhead, the motorway rumbled with the rush of cars into and out of the city. Water, or maybe some other liquid that Break had no desire to study, leaked down from the road and formed a sticky pool that the skaters did their best to avoid. It might look like a dump, but to him it was paradise.

'Alright, son?' Break's dad ambled over, tall and lean with the scars to prove that he'd done his time on the streets of London way back in the seventies.

Break sat on his board, watching the action. 'Yeah. Tired. You know.' Their conversations were never going to go on for hours.

'Well, I don't know whether to shake your hand or ground you for the next six months.' His dad frowned. 'If I'd have known the half of what you were up to...'

'But Charlie's my friend and...'

'You're a good lad, Arthur. You care and that's the point. Tell you what, if you do get up to any more insane adventures, whatever you do, please, please *don't* tell me. I might be a bloke, but I worry just as much as your mum.'

Break smiled, and his smile grew even wider as the rest of the gang turned up.

'Hey, Stu!' said Ben.

Break's dad nodded.

'How's it going?' said Break.

'Well, my dad's a free man,' Charlie answered. 'That's the main thing.' But the truth was that everyone looked washed out. A week had gone by since the night at Theodore's. Charlie, San, Break and Ben had been able to keep their parents in the dark up until they were all returned home in patrol cars, their blue lights flashing as if to let every single neighbour in on the secret. Fingers had been wagged, tears shed and all sorts of threats issued. But as the interviews proceeded over the next few days, anger was replaced with pride. Gossip about how their children were doing at school was replaced with the odd little boast, which incredulous parents took with a pinch of salt.

Vince had hired a QC to represent him, but even this well-paid figurehead of justice found the little problem of video evidence somewhat hard to deny. San also handed over the USB key – the final nail in the coffin with its footage of Vince prancing around the egg explaining its attributes to would-be buyers. For now, he was banged up on remand along with Piggy and Dirk. It meant that the gang didn't need eyes in the back of their heads each time they went out.

To protect the children, it was decided to put a press embargo on the whole situation. All the public knew was that the egg had been recovered and suspects arrested. According to the papers, a certain Theodore Perchin, great-grandson, etc., had been visiting the newly restored egg when he offered an explanation for the fine line that could be seen circling the egg from top to bottom. When the curator was summoned and the showcase opened, the egg once again cracked open under his expert hands. The hint of hidden romance and secret gemstones made page one and gave readers a break from the endless wars raging around the planet. Letters pages filled with speculation about the Empress and the goldsmith.

'How's Theodore?' asked Break.

'Enjoying all the publicity,' said Charlie. 'Everyone who is anyone wants to commission a real Fabergé fake from him. He's even been contacted by someone who claims to be the great-granddaughter of the Empress and her secret boyfriend!'

Everyone fell silent for a few seconds.

Ben spoke up. 'Well. We did it, didn't we?'

'Suppose so,' said San.

The silence deepened.

A police car screeched to a halt outside the gates. Break looked up to see his dad walk over to the driver's side. He nodded a couple of times and the officer got out of the car. Together they went to the back of the car and the policeman opened the boot. Break's dad pulled out a large bag and inspected the contents before heaving it over his shoulder. They carried on talking as Danny Cooper and Lance got out of the back.

'What's going on?' said Charlie. As the group made its way towards them, she recognised the officer with a sinking feeling. It was the man who'd arrested her dad in the first place.

'Here comes trouble!' hissed Ben. 'You'd think they'd leave us alone.'

The officer did not look happy at all. Danny nudged him. 'PC Smythe has something to say. Don't you?'

'Ermm. Yes. Well. You lot.'

'Go on,' said Danny.

'Right then. Apart from breaking and entering a business's premises, impersonating a solicitor to assist in a jail-cell break-out...'

Lance went bright red.

PC Smythe was on a roll. '...Using unlicensed vehicles in a public thoroughfare...'

'Does he mean *skateboards*?' whispered Charlie in Break's ear.

PC Smythe continued. '...Endangering pedestrians, damaging a police car, withholding evidence, not to mention taking the law into your own hands...'

Break's dad butted in. 'I think you've made your point.'

'Apart from all that, I have been asked by my superiors to officially...' – and Charlie could actually see the words stick in his throat – 'thank you for your work in solving this crime.' The man looked like he wanted to be anywhere but the spot he stood on. He shut his mouth, and his eyes stayed firmly stuck on a bit of chewing gum about two centimetres in front of his foot.

Break's dad opened the bag. 'Apparently these are for you,' he said with a big grin as four gleaming new boards tumbled onto the ground. 'They did ask me what the best kit was. So, here you go – Ricta Core Wheels, Swiss bearings, Venture trucks and Death decks all round.'

The PC turned to go.

Danny tapped him on the shoulder. 'Aren't we forgetting the best bit?'

PC Smythe reluctantly turned around and pulled an envelope out of his pocket.

'The Russian owner of the egg has written to you personally here. And there's a reward.' The officer held the envelope in his hand like a terrier. But he could see no way round it. He handed the letter to Charlie and scuttled off back to his car.

'Go on, open it!' said Danny.

Charlie was never one for doing what she was told. But this once, she did. She carefully unsealed the flap and pulled out the letter. She began to read.

Dear brave ones!

If I could confer honorary Russian citizenship on you, I would. I hope this small token may express my gratitude for returning what was lost and discovering what was hidden.

Yours, with unimaginable thanks,

Andrei Yevtushenko

A thin sliver of paper fluttered to the floor. Charlie bent to pick it up and her eyes nearly leapt from their sockets. 'No way!' It was time to get her mum out of that depressing bedroom and take the family for a proper break. She passed the cheque round.

'Now that's what I call a result!' said Ben, who started to imagine all the cities in which he could practice his free-running.

'Unbelievable!' agreed San, thinking of several gadgets even *Gizmoid* magazine could only dream about.

'Serious!' smiled Break, thinking of empty swimming pools and hot Californian sunshine.

'I'd better be included in this, after all you lot put me through!' insisted Lance. It would be great to finish drama school without debt. Maybe he could even put on the play he'd been secretly writing...

Danny Cooper leant over, snatched the cheque and folded it into his pocket. 'Before you fill your heads with fantasy, us adults will have a meeting to discuss how this reward should be divided and invested.'

The gang groaned. Typical parents. You do all the work and they get all the credit. But for now, there were more pressing matters to attend to. The boards were assessed by experienced hands and then let loose on the ramps and rails. As the afternoon wore on, the gang flew, slid, flipped and ground their way round the park. Even San tried out tricks he had only dreamt of. There were bone-crunching slams and impressive bailouts, scraped arms and a fair bit of blood as Break's dad gave them a hard time about the total lack of safety gear.

As the afternoon gave way into evening and the late sun lit up this hidden concrete den, Danny Cooper put on a spread to beat all spreads in the chill-out zone. The food was good, the jokes were bad.

'School next week,' said Ben, in a voice the opposite of happy.

'Don't remind me!' said Charlie. But with all they'd been through, school would be a piece of cake.

'Of course, we'll have to ignore you in the school yard! Can't be seen associating with a *girl* in the year below.'

'Thanks, Ben. It's so nice to be appreciated! Next time you want your life saved, don't call me!' Charlie paused for a second as she stuffed down her third helping of homemade pizza. 'I was thinking. Maybe we should hire ourselves out? You know?'

'But what would we call ourselves? Team of kids with specialist talents? Own transport supplied?' said Break. 'It hardly trips off the tongue.'

'I've got it!' said San. 'How about...the Skateboard Detectives?'

Ben nearly choked on his Coke. 'Now that, my friends, is absolutely priceless!'

Don't miss the gang's next action-packed adventure!

THE SKATEBOARD DETECTIVES

DIAMONDS ARE FOR EVIL

Coming soon . . .

1 FLIGHT

Saturday 29 September, 2.45 am — the present

Break shuffled up to the ledge of the flat roof, pulled back his hood and peered over. The face that checked out the very long way down was framed by a mop of black hair. The skin was pale and hinted at too much food with a high grease content. Brown eyes nervously scanned the scene, looking for trouble.

Four storeys below, the shop fronts were shuttered and bolted. By day, this pedestrianised alley thronged with the rich and wannabe wealthy, looking to make the deal of a lifetime. Now there was only a staggering drunk, busy recycling his dinner onto the pavement. The man stumbled off and the gang were ready to go.

'No way,' Break hissed. Heights were not his thing.

Ben's rangy form curled up in the corner, trying not to shiver. 'What do you mean?' he whispered back. 'You've done it before.'

'Falling into a river is one thing, but ending up as the filling in a concrete sandwich is another.' Break put his skateboard down and started scratching the scabs on his elbow. He'd popped some decent air in his time, but this was suicidal. His last jump had been a smooth nollie off a set of twelve steps. The move was good, and he even managed to land at the bottom with a textbook tail manual. That's when it all went wrong: Hitting the ground with two wheels followed by a perfect bloody elbow slide. Bad bailout. He had no desire to repeat the experience.

'Stop squabbling you two,' said Charlie, with an exasperated look on her face. 'The point is, how do we get over...?'

More Orchard books you might enjoy

The Howling Tower	Michael Coleman	978 1 84362 938 2	£4.99
The Fighting Pit	Michael Coleman	978 1 84616 214 5	£5.99
The Hunting Forest	Michael Coleman	978 1 84616 044 8	£5.99
The Fire Within	Chris d'Lacey	978 1 84121 533 4	£5.99
Icefire	Chris d'Lacey	978 1 84362 134 8	£5.99
Fire Star	Chris d'Lacey	978 1 84362 522 3	£5.99
The Haunting of Nathaniel Wolfe	Brian Keaney	978 1 84616 520 7	£5.99
The Poltergoose	Michael Lawrence	978 1 86039 836 0	£4.99
The Killer Underpants	Michael Lawrence	978 1 84121 713 0	£5.99
The Iron, the Switch and the Broom Cupboard	Michael Lawrence	978 1 84616 471 2	£5.99

Orchard books are available from all good bookshops, or can be ordered direct from the publisher: Orchard Books, PO BOX 29, Douglas IM99 1BQ

Credit card orders please telephone 01624 836000
or fax 01624 837033 or visit our website:
www.orchardbooks.co.uk or email:
bookshop@enterprise.net for details.

To order please quote title, author and ISBN
and your full name and address.
Cheques and postal orders should be made payable
to 'Bookpost plc'.
Postage and packing is FREE within the UK
(overseas customers should add £1.00 per book).

Prices and availability are subject to change.